Violet glanced at her watch again as Landon came back with the coffee.

"Still timing me?" he asked, sitting down.

"No. I was just thinking that there's a call I should make soon."

"Go ahead, if you want."

He might be making an effort to be accommodating. Or he might be interested in who she was calling. She hadn't quite made up her mind yet about Mr. Landon Derringer.

"I'll wait until I've seen your mysterious friend," she said.

He glanced at the door. "You won't have long to wait. She's here."

The door swung open, and a woman stepped inside. Slim, chic, sophisticated. And other than that, Violet's exact double.

* * *

Texas Twins: Two sets of twins, torn apart by family secrets, find their way home.

Her Surprise Sister—Marta Perry
July 2012

Mirror Image Bride—Barbara McMahon
August 2012

Carbon Copy Cowboy—Arlene James
September 2012

Look-Alike Lawman—Glynna Kaye
October 2012

The Soldier's Newfound Family—Kathryn Springer
November 2012

Reunited for the Holidays—Jillian Hart
December 2012

Books by Marta Perry

Love Inspired

Hunter's Bride
**A Mother's Wish*
**A Time to Forgive*
**Promise Forever*
Always in Her Heart
The Doctor's Christmas
True Devotion
†*Hero in Her Heart*
†*Unlikely Hero*
†*Hero Dad*
†*Her Only Hero*
†*Hearts Afire*
†*Restless Hearts*
†*A Soldier's Heart*
Mission: Motherhood
***Twice in a Lifetime*
***Heart of the Matter*
***The Guardian's Honor*
***Mistletoe Prayers*
"The Bodine Family Christmas"
Her Surprise Sister

Love Inspired Suspense

**Tangled Memories*
Season of Secrets
††*Hide in Plain Sight*
††*A Christmas to Die For*
††*Buried Sins*
Final Justice
Twin Targets

*Caldwell Kin
†The Flanagans
**The Bodine Family
††The Three Sisters Inn

MARTA PERRY

has written everything from Sunday-school curricula to travel articles to magazine stories in more than twenty years of writing, but she feels she's found her writing home in the stories she writes for the Love Inspired lines.

Marta lives in rural Pennsylvania, but she and her husband spend part of each year at their second home in South Carolina. When she's not writing, she's probably visiting her children and her six beautiful grandchildren, traveling, gardening or relaxing with a good book.

Marta loves hearing from readers, and she'll write back with a signed bookmark and/or her brochure of Pennsylvania Dutch recipes. Write to her c/o Love Inspired Books, 233 Broadway, Suite 1001, New York, NY 10279, email her at marta@martaperry.com, or visit her on the web at www.martaperry.com.

Her Surprise Sister

Marta Perry

Love Inspired

Special thanks and acknowledgement to Marta Perry for her participation in the Texas Twins miniseries.

Recycling programs for this product may not exist in your area.

ISBN-13: 978-0-373-87752-2

HER SURPRISE SISTER

This edition published by arrangement with Love Inspired Books.

www.LoveInspiredBooks.com

Printed in U.S.A.

When I look at thy heavens, the work of thy fingers,
the moon and the stars which thou hast established,
what is man, that thou should remember him, or
mortal man, that thou should care for him?

—*Psalms* 8:3–4

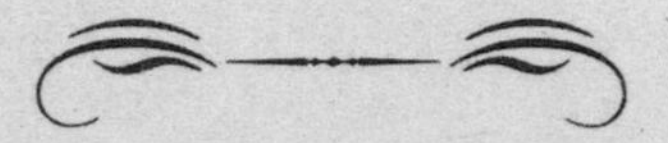

This story is dedicated to the Love Inspired sisters
who worked on this continuity series.
And, as always, to Brian, with much love.

Chapter One

What could she possibly say to a father who had walked out of her life when she was an infant? *Hi, Dad, it's me, Violet?*

Violet Colby's fingers tightened on the steering wheel. What was she doing miles from home in Fort Worth, trying to follow an almost nonexistent clue to her birth father?

A sleek sports car cut in front of her SUV, horn blaring. Shaken, Violet flipped on the turn signal and pulled into the right lane. City traffic had frazzled whatever nerves she had left.

A coffee-shop sign ahead beckoned to her. That was what she needed—a short respite, a jolt of caffeine and a chance to reassess her situation.

She found a parking space, fed the meter and pushed open the coffee shop's glass door, fatigue dragging at her. The aroma drew her irresistibly in, and a few moments later she was sitting at a small round glass table, a steaming mug and a flaky croissant in front of her. She hadn't bothered to read through the long list of specialty coffees the shop offered. All she wanted was caffeine, the sooner the better.

A woman brushed past her, the summer-print dress and high platform sandals she wore making Violet uncomfortably aware of her faded jeans and scuffed cowboy boots. It wasn't that she hadn't been in Fort Worth before, but she usually took the time to dress appropriately for a trip to the city, a five-hour drive from the Colby Ranch. This time she'd bolted out of her mother's hospital room, exhausted from long nights of waiting and praying for her mom to open her eyes.

She hadn't been able to take it any longer. That wasn't the Belle Colby everyone in the county knew, lying there motionless day after day. Belle Colby was energetic, vibrant, always in motion. She had to be, running a spread the size of the Colby Ranch and raising two kids on her own.

Not now. Not since her mare had stepped in a hole, sending Belle crashing to the ground. And Jack, Violet's big brother, was so eaten up with guilt for arguing with their mom before the accident that he was being no help at all.

Violet broke a corner off the croissant and nibbled at it. Her family was broken, it seemed, and she was the only one who could fix it. That's what she'd been thinking during those lonely hours before dawn at her mother's hospital bed. The only solution her tired brain could come up with was to find their father—the man Belle never talked about.

Now that she was here in Fort Worth, where she'd been born, the task seemed futile. Worse, it seemed stupid. What would it accomplish if she did find him?

She didn't belong here, any more than the sophisticated-looking guy coming in the door would belong on the ranch. Swanky suit and designer tie, glossy leather boots that had certainly never been worn to muck out a stall, a Stetson with not a smudge to mar its perfection—he was big-city Texas, that was for sure.

That man's head turned, as if he felt her stare, and she caught the full impact of a pair of icy green eyes before she could look away. She stared down at her coffee. Quickly she raised the mug, hoping to hide her embarrassment at being caught gaping.

It didn't seem to be working. She heard approaching footsteps and kept her gaze down. A pair of glossy brown boots moved into her range of vision.

"What are you doing here?"

Violet looked up, surprised. "What?"

"I said, what are you doing here?" He pulled out the chair opposite her, uninvited, and sat down. "I told you I'd be at your apartment…" He slid back the sleeve of his suit to consult the gold watch on his tanned wrist. "In five minutes. So why are you in the coffee shop instead of at your condo? Are you trying to avoid me?"

Okay, he was crazy. That was the only answer Violet could come up with. She groped for her bag, keeping her eyes on his face. It looked sane enough, with a deep tan that made those green eyes bright in contrast, a square, stubborn-looking jaw, and a firm mouth. His expensively cut hair was sandy blond.

He didn't *look* crazy, but what did that mean? Or maybe this was his idea of a pick-up line.

Her fingers closed on her bag and she started to rise. His hand shot across the table and closed around her wrist. Not hard, but firmly enough that she couldn't pull away without an undignified struggle.

"The least you can do is talk to me about it." He looked as if keeping his temper was an effort. "Whatever you think, I still want to marry you."

Violet sent a panicked glance around the coffee shop.

The customers had cleared out and even the barista had disappeared into the back. People walked by on the sidewalk outside, but they were oblivious to the drama being played out.

"Well?" He sounded impatient.

Her own temper spiked. "Well, *what?* Are you crazy?" That probably wasn't the smartest thing to say, but it was what she felt. "Let go of me right now before I yell the place down."

His grip loosened and he looked at her, puzzlement creeping into his eyes. "Maddie? Why are you acting this way? What's wrong?"

Relief made her limp for an instant. He wasn't crazy. He'd mistaken her for someone else.

A flicker of caution shot through her relief. If this someone else was a woman he'd proposed to, how could he mistake Violet for her?

"My name isn't Maddie." She said the words in a soft, even tone, the way she'd speak to a half-gentled horse. Maybe it worked on humans, too. "I think you've confused me with someone else."

His fingers still encircling her wrist loosely, he studied her, letting his gaze move from her hair, probably escaping from the scrunchy she'd put on her ponytail ages ago, to a face that was undoubtedly bare of makeup at this stage of the day, to her Western shirt and well-worn jeans.

Finally he shook his head. "You're not Maddie Wallace, are you?"

"No. I'm not." She pulled her wrist free. "Now that we have that straight, I'll be going...."

"Wait." He made a grab for her wrist again, and then seemed to think the better of it when she raised her fist.

"I'm sorry." He gave her a rueful, disarming grin. "You must think I'm crazy."

"The thought did cross my mind." A smile like his would charm the birds from the trees. Maybe it was worth sitting still another minute for. She had to admit, she was curious.

"It's uncanny." A line formed between his eyebrows. "But I think..." He let that sentence fade away. "Look, my name is Landon Derringer. Here's my card." He slid a business card from his pocket and put it on the table in front of her. According to the card, Landon Derringer was the CEO of an outfit called Derringer Investments.

Of course, that didn't prove anything. "Not that I'm skeptical, but I could have a business card made up that said I was the queen of England."

He chuckled, the sound a bass rumble that seemed to vibrate, sending a faint tingle along her skin. "Fair enough. But if you'll be patient for a few minutes while I make a call, I think you'll find it worthwhile."

She gave him an assessing gaze. Her brother would probably say she was naive to trust this guy, but then Jack and everybody else at Colby Ranch tended to treat her as if she were about ten. Oddly enough, that decided it for her.

"All right."

The guy—Landon—gave a crisp nod. "Good." He flipped open a cell phone.

In normal circumstances she would think it impolite to listen to someone else's phone conversation. But nothing about this encounter was normal, and she intended to hear what he said. This encounter had one thing going for it: it had taken her mind off her troubles, at least briefly.

"Maddie? This is Landon. Just listen, will you?"

This Maddie person must not be eager to talk to him, judging by his tone.

"I'm over at the Coffee Stop, and there's someone here you have to meet. I think she might have some answers about that odd package you received last week."

He paused while she talked, and Violet could hear the light notes of a female voice, but not the words.

"No, this is not just an excuse to see you." He sounded as if he were trying to hold on to his patience.

More waiting, while the voice went on.

"Okay," he said finally. "Right. We'll be here."

He clicked off, and then met Violet's raised eyebrows with another flash of that smile. "Five minutes. It won't take her any longer than that to get here. Her apartment is just down the street a block or so. And you'll find meeting her interesting, I promise."

She glanced at her watch. "Okay. I'll give you five minutes, no more."

"Good." He rose, taking her coffee mug. "I'll get you a refill. And you look as if you could use something a little more substantial than that croissant."

"What do you—"

But he'd already gone to the counter. She was tempted to pull out a mirror and look at herself, but that would betray the fact that she cared what he thought. Anyone would look frazzled after as many sleepless nights as she'd had.

She glanced at her watch again as he came back with the coffee.

"Still timing me?" he asked, sitting down.

"No. I was just thinking that there's a call I should make soon." She'd have to check in at the hospital to see if there'd been any change. And try to track her brother down, if she could.

"Go ahead, if you want."

He might be making an effort to be accommodating. Or he might be interested in who she was calling. She hadn't quite made up her mind yet about Mr. Landon Derringer.

"I'll wait until I've seen your mysterious friend," she said.

He glanced at the door. "You won't have long to wait. She's here."

The door swung open and a woman stepped inside. Slim, chic, sophisticated. And other than that, Violet's exact double. Violet's breath stopped. It was like being thrown from a horse, the wind knocked out of her. This couldn't be true, but it was. The evidence stood right in front of her.

Landon rose as Maddie turned toward them. She took a step, her cautious smile fading as she looked from Landon to his companion. Her eyes widened; her face paled.

"Maddie, are you all right?" He kicked himself mentally. He should have given her more of a warning.

She nodded and walked toward them as slowly as if she were wading through water. When she reached the table, he pulled a chair out and she sank into it, never taking her eyes from the other woman's face.

He was having a bit of difficulty with that himself. He looked from one to the other, feeling almost dizzy. Same long, straight auburn hair, same chocolate-brown eyes, same delicate features. Aside from the obvious differences in style and clothing, it was like looking at mirror images.

"Who are you?" Maddie ignored him when she spoke, all her attention on the other woman. He'd been careful not to ask the woman's name, since she'd clearly been suspicious of him, and he waited, curious, to see how she responded to Maddie.

"Violet Colby." She said the name, seeming perplexed for a moment, as if wondering if she really were who she thought she was.

Small wonder. How could anyone react when confronted by an exact duplicate?

The stranger—Violet—seemed to shake herself, as if in an effort to regain control. "Who are you? Why..." She glanced from Maddie to Landon. "Is this a trick of some kind?" Her voice sharpened with suspicion as she looked at him.

"How could it be a trick?" he asked, spreading his hands to indicate innocence. "When I saw you sitting here, I thought you were Maddie. You're identical. I couldn't make that up."

Curiously, Maddie's expression was equally suspicious as she looked at her duplicate. "I don't believe it. Are you the person who sent me that note?"

Violet looked confused. She shook her head, the long ponytail swinging, tendrils of hair freeing themselves to cluster on her neck. Maddie hadn't worn her hair that way since she was about fourteen, when she was in the middle of her horse-mania stage. It made him feel for a moment as if Violet were a kid.

Careful, he warned himself. *You don't know anything about this woman, and Maddie's family has money and position.* This could be some sort of elaborate scam, and if so, it was his duty to protect Maddie. He'd promised her brother he'd look after her.

When Maddie didn't speak, Violet seemed to feel more of a response was called for. "I don't know what you're talking about. What note? How could I send you anything when I didn't even know you existed until just this moment?"

They could go on dancing around the question all day, it seemed. He'd always rather go straight to the heart of the matter.

"Look, it's obvious that you two are identical twins. Just look at yourselves. Maddie, did you bring the note?"

He expected a flare-up from Maddie at his assumption of authority, but she just nodded and fished in her bag. The shock of this encounter seemed to have knocked the stuffing out of her for the moment.

Maddie drew out a much-creased piece of notepaper and pushed it across the table. Violet spread the note flat and bent over to read it.

Landon didn't need to look at the page again to know what the note said. The words had been revolving in his mind since Maddie received it a couple of weeks ago.

I am sorry for what I did to you and your family. I hope you and your siblings, especially your twin, can forgive me as I ask the Lord to forgive me.

No signature, and the ink was a bit faded, as if it hadn't been written recently.

"I don't understand," Violet said, pushing the paper back to Maddie. "Where did this come from? Why would you think I had anything to do with it?"

"Because you're obviously the twin referred to in the note," he said, watching her closely. But he couldn't see any indication that she was faking. Her puzzlement and distress seemed natural.

"Let me tell it," Maddie said, interrupting. "It's my business."

Not yours, in other words. But he couldn't be pushed

away so easily. In the absence of her father and brothers, Maddie needed someone to watch over her, even though she didn't think she did.

"This letter appeared in my mailbox a couple of weeks ago." Maddie touched the note. "It was tucked into a new Bible, with no indication of who it was from." She shrugged. "It upset me at first. It seemed so weird. But then I assumed it had just been sent to the wrong person. I don't have a twin." She paused. "Anyway, I didn't think so."

"I didn't think so, either." Violet paused. "They do say that everyone has a double somewhere. Maybe it's just some sort of odd…" Her voice died off, probably because she realized how ridiculous that was.

"The obvious solution is usually the right one," Landon said. If he didn't keep pushing, they'd never come to a conclusion. "Would you mind telling us about your family, Violet? If you were adopted—"

She was already shaking her head. "I know what you're thinking, that we could have been split up as babies and adopted by different couples. But it can't be. Everyone says I look just like my mother." A shadow crossed her face when she spoke of her mother…distress, fear…he wasn't sure what.

"What is it?" He reached impulsively for her hand. "Is something wrong with your mother?"

Violet took a deep breath, seeming to draw some sort of invisible armor around her. "My mother was in an accident a few days ago. She had a bad fall from a horse. She's been in a coma in a trauma center in Amarillo ever since."

"I'm sorry." The depth of her pain touched him, even though she was trying to hide it. "But…what are you doing here in Fort Worth, then?"

Violet's lips trembled for an instant before she summoned up control. "I…it was a crazy idea, I guess. But I thought maybe I could find my father."

"Find your father?" Now it was Maddie's voice that shook a little. "Is he missing?"

Violet rubbed her temples, and he thought she was fighting tears. "I don't know. I've never known who my father was. I was sitting there in the hospital, praying that Mom would open her eyes, and suddenly I was longing to see my father." She gave a shaky laugh. "I suppose I wanted someone to walk in and tell me it was going to be all right. Stupid, isn't it?"

"Maybe not so stupid," he said. "It brought you here, didn't it? But why Fort Worth?"

"Because this is where I was born. My mother did tell my brother that when he kept badgering her about it, although then she closed up and wouldn't say any more. I thought I might find some records."

"Do you know which hospital?" At least that was something that could be checked. Landon would welcome some positive task that would lead to unraveling this puzzle.

Violet shook her head. "Mom always clammed up whenever we asked her about it. So eventually I stopped asking. My brother, Jack, was more interested in finding out than I was, but she just always said we were better off not knowing."

"I can run a check on hospital records. What's your birthday?" He pulled out his cell phone. The firm of private investigators his company sometimes used would know how to access that information.

"January 26th." They made the reply almost in unison, and then looked at each other, some sort of bond seeming to form in that moment.

"You don't need to do any checking," Maddie said. "It's obvious, as you said. We're sisters." She reached across the table, touching Violet's hand. They looked at each other, faces breaking into identical smiles.

It couldn't help but warm his heart, but his rational mind sounded a note of caution. All they knew about this woman was what she'd told them.

A couple of college boys came into the coffee shop, discussing baseball loudly as they approached the counter. Maddie gave them an annoyed look.

"We can't talk here," she said. "Violet, you just have to come back to my condo. There are a million things I want to ask you. All right? Will you come?"

Violet seemed to hesitate for a moment. Then she nodded. "Okay."

Landon rose when they did, and Maddie gave him what was obviously a dismissive smile.

"Thank you, Landon. I appreciate what you did to bring us together. I'll talk with you sometime soon." She turned away, heading for the door.

Violet was obviously startled by Maddie's action. She started to follow and then turned back, giving him a shy smile.

"Thank you, Landon. If I hadn't run into you, I might never have known I have a twin." She held out her hand, and he took it.

They stood for a moment, hands clasped, and it seemed to him they were making a promise. Confused by the sudden emotion, he smiled and stepped back. He'd been summarily dismissed, and he couldn't very well barge into Maddie's condo to see what they did next.

But as he watched them walk out the door together, he knew this couldn't be the end of his involvement. Even if Violet were as genuine as she seemed, the situation still had the potential to explode, hurting the whole Wallace family. And if Violet were playing some game of her own…

Well, even though their engagement had never been more than a formality, it was his duty to protect Maddie, and that was what he intended to do.

Chapter Two

Violet hurried outside to catch up with Maddie, her palm still tingling from Landon's touch. That wouldn't do, she lectured herself. According to the dapper CEO, he wanted to marry Maddie.

Still wanted, he'd said. That implied there'd been an engagement between them, didn't it? So what had gone wrong for them?

On the face of it, Landon Derringer was quite a guy—obviously handsome and sophisticated, apparently wealthy and successful. Still, Maddie knew him better than she did. There could be very good reasons why she'd changed her mind about marrying him.

Maddie waited on the busy sidewalk and gestured down the street. This part of Fort Worth seemed to be a mix of businesses, professional offices and apartment buildings.

"My condo is only a couple of blocks from here, so I walked. But maybe you want to take your car and park it there in the garage, rather than leave it on the street."

"Yes, thanks." Violet went quickly to the SUV and opened the door to be greeted by a blast of heat. Texas-in-July heat. She switched on the ignition, turned the air on full blast, and rolled the windows down as Maddie got in. "Sorry it's so stifling. It should cool off pretty fast."

"No problem. I was born here, remember? I'm used to it." Maddie shook her head, her silky hair swaying. She wore it in a shoulder-length cut that had obviously been done by a professional, since the style fell back into place with every movement.

Violet couldn't help touching her ponytail. Would her hair look that way with the right cut? Maybe so, but she couldn't afford to find out. Anyway, the ponytail was a lot more practical for the life she led.

She checked the rearview mirror and pulled out into traffic. In the mirror she could also glimpse Landon Derringer, still standing by the coffee-shop door.

"We both were born here," Violet said, still trying to understand what was happening to her. "Do you think your friend will really be able to find the records?"

"Probably. He has the connections, if anyone does." Maddie's nose crinkled. "I wish he'd butt out, but knowing Landon, he won't."

Violet hesitated for a moment before asking the question in her mind. "When he first saw me, Landon thought I was you. He said he still wanted to marry me. You, I mean." She was probably blushing.

Maddie shrugged, a quick, graceful movement. "I ought to tell you about it, I guess. Landon and I were engaged, but it was a mistake. Now we're not. End of story."

It couldn't be all there was. Violet knew there had to be a lot more to the engagement and the breakup than that, but if Maddie didn't want to tell her, she wouldn't pry.

"Just past this next corner," Maddie said. "Turn right into the basement garage."

Violet followed her directions, turning into an underground parking garage. She parked the car where Maddie indicated and walked beside her, their footsteps echoing on the concrete floor. They stepped into an elevator that lifted them soundlessly to the third floor.

"Right over here." Maddie pulled out keys as she spoke, going quickly down the carpeted hallway to the second door. She unlocked it and led the way into a condo.

So this fancy place was where her twin lived. It looked like a magazine spread.

"This is lovely." Violet stepped into the living room, which had a dining area on one end and an open counter, beyond which was a small kitchen. Spacious and trendy, with sleek leather furniture and vibrant paintings on the walls, the living room had a bank of glass doors leading onto a balcony that overlooked the city.

Maddie looked around, as if surprised by her comment. "I guess it is. Dad helped me buy this place when I decided to get out on my own."

Dad. The casual word echoed in Violet's mind. Was Maddie's father her father, too? He must be, for them to be identical twins. She realized she was still trying to wrap her mind around that one fact.

"What's your father like?"

Maddie crossed the Berber carpet to a glass-topped table that held a series of photos in silver frames. She picked one up, holding it out.

Violet took the photo and stared at three pictured faces. The older man had to be Maddie's father. *Her father.* He had a chiseled face and dark brown eyes with a somber expression. Remote—that was how he looked.

The other two were younger. She stared at one of the pictured faces and felt the room spin around.

"Who is that?" She pointed to the face.

Maddie looked at her oddly. “Are you okay? That’s just my older brother, Grayson.”

Violet shook her head, pulling her cell phone out of her bag and flipping through the photos until she found the one she wanted. “This is my older brother, Jack.” She handed it to Maddie, knowing she’d see what Violet meant at once. The faces were identical.

Maddie stared at the photo for a long moment. She sank down onto the nearest sofa, looking shell-shocked. “I feel as if I’ve wandered into a science-fiction movie.”

Violet sat down next to her. “Me, too. Two sets of identical twins? It’s…it’s just crazy.”

“That’s the right word for it,” Maddie agreed, shaking her head in disbelief.

“Who is the other person?” Violet pointed to the third man in the framed photo.

“My younger brother, Carter.” Maddie looked at her. “Please don’t tell me you have an identical younger brother. That would be too much. I’d be ready for the funny farm.”

Violet managed a smile. “I don’t have any younger siblings at all.”

“That’s a relief.” Maddie flushed. “I mean…I didn’t mean that I’m glad you don’t have younger siblings. Or that I’m not glad to have found you. It’s just…”

“Yes. I know.” Violet rubbed her forehead. Maybe if she weren’t so tired, she could think this through better. “So what do we make of this? We must have the same parents in order to be identical, to say nothing of Jack and Grayson being identical. So my mother and your dad were together at one time, and they had two sets of twins. That’s what we’re saying, isn’t it?”

“I guess so.” Maddie was staring at the photo she’d identified as being her younger brother. “But that must mean Carter is my half brother. I remember when he was born. It never occurred to me that Mom wasn't my mother, too."

Violet could hear the hurt in Maddie's voice, and it seemed to echo in her heart. There were too many complications for her to grapple with. "What about your dad? He has to know the answers to this. Can't we go and see him?" Her heart gave an extra thump at the thought of actually seeing her birth father.

But Maddie was shaking her head. "He's not within reach, I'm afraid. Dad's a doctor. Right now he's on a mission trip, and he said he wouldn't be in cell-phone range most of the time. Not that we talk all that much, anyway." Maddie shrugged. "If you're picturing an old-fashioned, doting, emotionally engaged father, forget it. Dad's more involved with his patients than with his kids."

"I'm sorry." She reached out to touch Maddie's hand, responding to the pain in her voice. "But there must be some way of reaching him in an emergency. We'll go nuts if we don't find some answers."

"I can send an email. He is able to pick those up occasionally. But before I do that, tell me about your mother. *Our* mother. You said we look like her."

Violet flipped through the cell phone photos again, stopping at one she especially liked. Belle was leaning against a corral fence, wearing her usual jeans, plaid shirt and boots, her head tilted back, smiling with that pleasure she always seemed to take in whatever she was doing at the moment. Violet touched the image. She'd give a lot to see her mom looking like that again. She handed the phone to Maddie.

"Oh." Maddie touched the image, just as Violet had. She wiped away a tear. "We are like her, aren't we? It's funny to look at her and know what I'll look like in twenty years or so. She's beautiful."

"Yes. But right now—"

"You said she'd been in an accident." Maddie rushed her words. "How bad is it?"

"Bad." Violet swallowed the tears that wanted to spill out. "Her horse stepped in a hole, and she fell. Mom has a head injury. They were able to get help right away, but it was serious." Her voice thickened. "At first they didn't think she'd live, but she was tough enough to survive the surgery. Now…well, now they don't know if she'll ever wake up."

Maddie's hand closed on hers, the grip tight and imperative. "I have to see her. Please, Violet. She's my mother, and I've never seen her, and if she doesn't make it…" Her voice broke. "Can I go back with you?"

The enormity of the request hit Violet. If she took Maddie home with her, took her to see her mom, how on earth was she going to explain her?

"I know what you're thinking," Maddie said softly. "That would bring this craziness out in the open for sure. But if I don't see her—"

"It's okay." She'd figure out the explanations somehow. "Why don't you pack a bag? You can follow me back to the ranch. You probably want your own car there."

Maddie jumped to her feet. "It won't take me a minute. Make yourself at home. Help yourself to the fridge. You must be tired and hungry."

She was, probably too tired to drive all that way, but she didn't really have a choice. She couldn't stay away any longer, relying on other people to run the ranch and look after her mother.

She scouted through the contents of the refrigerator,

feeling a little odd to be helping herself. But that was what Maddie had said, and she did need something to keep her going. Maddie's tastes seemed to run to fresh fruit and cheeses, judging by her fridge.

Maddie was back in minutes, carrying a suitcase.

"That was fast." Violet was still eating the yogurt she'd found on the top shelf. It was lemon, her favorite, making her wonder if she and Maddie had similar tastes.

"I used to travel for my job, so I got pretty good at packing in a hurry." Maddie glanced toward the laptop on a corner desk. "I'll email Dad, just telling him it's important that he contact me right away. And I guess I'd better email Landon as well. I'll take my laptop with me so I can stay in touch."

Violet waited, trying not to look interested in what Maddie was typing. It was obvious that Maddie still cared about Landon, or she wouldn't be letting him know what was going on. Probably their broken engagement would be mended eventually. Someday she might be taking a part in her sister's wedding.

Violet was unpleasantly surprised to discover that she felt an odd twinge at the thought of Landon and Maddie getting married.

Violet and Maddie drove straight through to the ranch, stopping only to eat once. Maddie wanted to go right to the hospital, but once Violet had found there was no change in her mother's condition, she knew she had to get a decent night's sleep.

Relief flooded through her when she finally drove through the imposing stone gateway to the Colby Ranch. The three entwined *C*s at the top of the gate's arch seemed to welcome her home.

She pulled up in front of the sprawling brick-and-stone structure that was the main house, aware of Maddie's car behind her. When she still hadn't been able to reach Jack, Violet had phoned Lupita, the housekeeper, cook and second mother who kept the house running like a well-oiled machine, telling her to prepare the guest room.

Violet hadn't said whom she was bringing. The effort to explain over the phone had seemed way too much to her. Thank goodness Lupita, with her usual gentle wisdom probably sensing that questions weren't welcome, hadn't asked.

"This is it," she said as Maddie joined her on the wide front porch.

"It's huge." Maddie glanced around. Mature trees and a wrought-iron fence surrounded the ranch house, with grasslands and rolling hills stretching out in the distance. Behind the house, outbuildings dotted the property: barns, greenhouses, storage sheds, the cottages occupied by Lupita and her husband and that of foreman Ty Garland, and the bunkhouses. Colby Ranch was a busy place, so busy that it was sometimes hard to find a moment alone.

"I'll show you around tomorrow." She picked up Maddie's suitcase. "Right now let's get you settled and see what Lupita's fixed for supper."

"I think you're the one who needs to settle." Maddie linked her arm with Violet's. "You've been running at full speed since the accident, haven't you?"

"Pretty much." Violet pushed open the heavy oak front door and led Maddie into the center hallway. The pale tiled floor gleamed in the fading light, and there were fresh flowers, as always, on the massive oak credenza against the side wall. The staircase swept upward to the second floor in front of them. Through the glass doors at the far back end of the hallway, solar lights cast a glow over the courtyard.

"I'm home," Violet called as she always did when she entered the house. "Lupita, are you here?"

"*Sí, sí,* I'm coming." Lupita emerged from the kitchen at the back of the house, wiping her hands on the apron she'd wrapped around her plump waist. "It's about time you were getting home." The tone was gently scolding and filled with love. "You must—"

Another step, and she had seen Maddie. She stopped, black eyes wide and questioning, and Violet thought she murmured a prayer in Spanish.

"Lupita, this is Maddie Wallace." What else could she say?

Fortunately, there seemed no need. Lupita rushed to them and wrapped her arms around Violet, enfolding her in a loving hug. "So," she said softly. "I was right. There was a sister."

Violet pulled back, thoughts tumbling. "You knew I had a sister? Lupita, how could you keep this from me?"

"No, no, I didn't know." She patted Violet's cheek. "Don't fuss, little one. Once when your mother was sick, she rambled. She spoke of her baby girls, calling for them. So I thought there had been another. But I never thought to see her, not in this life."

"You thought I had a sister that died," Violet said, suddenly understanding.

Lupita nodded, turning to Maddie. She walked to her, taking Maddie's face in her hands and studying her for a long moment. "You are home," she said. "I am glad."

She turned, reverting to briskness probably to hide her emotion. "You must be starved, both of you. Wash up and get to the table. The food will be there by the time you are." She bustled back to the kitchen, wiping her eyes with the tea towel she held.

Maddie looked a little dazed. She put her hand to her cheek. "I didn't expect that kind of a welcome."

"Lupita's been with us since we were kids. As far as she's concerned, we're her kids, too."

"Do you think she knows anything more about us?" Maddie set her bag on the credenza. "Wouldn't she have tried to find out more from your mother, if it happened as she said?"

Violet shrugged. "Lupita always tells the truth, but sometimes she leaves things out. For our own good, she'd say. If she knows anything else about us, I'll get it out of her eventually."

By the time Lupita had stuffed them full of her special chicken enchiladas with black beans and rice, topped off with a scrumptious peach tart, Violet was feeling vaguely human again. She leaned back in her seat. Lupita always said that trouble and an empty belly were bad companions, and this time she seemed to be right. But even though she felt better, Violet was still too conscious of the empty chairs at the table.

Maddie, who'd demolished her piece of peach tart, was staring at the framed portrait on the dining room wall. "Who is that? Another relative?"

"That's Uncle James." Violet smiled at the pictured face, the weathering and wisdom of years showing in skin like crinkled leather. Kind blue eyes seemed to smile back at her. "James Crawford. He wasn't actually a relative, but that's what Jack and I always called him."

"Who was he, then?" Maddie eyed the portrait curiously.

"He owned this place. Mom came here as housekeeper

when I was three and Jack was five. He took us in and made us feel as if this was our home, too. He didn't have any family, and soon he was treating us like kin. I really don't even remember a time when he wasn't part of our lives."

"So he left this place to you?" Maddie sounded faintly disapproving.

"Not just like that," Violet responded, sensitive to criticism on that subject. Other people had talked about that, she felt sure, but Belle had ignored them. "Over the years, Uncle James needed more and more help. Mom took over the bookkeeping, and as his health failed, she took on increased responsibility for every aspect of the ranch. Eventually Uncle James insisted on making her a partner, and when he died, we found that he'd left the rest to her."

Violet's confidence faltered. Had Uncle James known the truth about them? Had he known about their twins? She suspected that even if he'd been privy to her mom's secret, he never would have told. Honor was everything to a man like Uncle James.

Violet pushed her chair back as one of Lupita's numerous nieces came in with a tray, the young woman's gaze wide-eyed and curious when she looked at Maddie. Word of this event would be all over the ranch in minutes and all over the county in a day. Violet was resigned to that happening.

"Let's take our tea into the living room so we're out of Lupita's way." She stifled a yawn. "I hope..."

Her voice faded as she heard boots coming from the direction of the kitchen. She rose from her chair. If only it was Jack...

But it wasn't. Ty Garland, the ranch foreman, paused in the hallway, hat in his hands.

"Sorry to bother you, Violet." He seemed to be making an effort not to look at Maddie, which meant he'd already heard about her arrival. "I was hoping you knew when Jack would be around. There's a couple of things I need to talk to him about."

"I wish I knew the answer to that, too, Ty." She glanced toward Maddie to find her looking at Ty appreciatively. Maybe Maddie was practically engaged, but she certainly noticed the tall, dark and handsome Ty.

Sighing, Violet decided she'd better make introductions.

"Maddie, this is Ty Garland, our foreman. Ty, this is my…this is Maddie Wallace."

Ty nodded, falling silent as he did so readily, especially with strangers. And Maddie, with her elegant looks and bearing, was definitely different from anyone around here.

"It's nice to meet you, Ty." Maddie smiled up at him from where she sat. "It sounds as if you have a lot of responsibility around here."

"Yes, ma'am." Ty eyed Maddie warily, making Violet wonder what he was thinking.

Maybe she'd better get this conversation back to business. "What was it you needed to talk to Jack about?"

Ty turned to her with something like relief in his dark eyes. "Well, for starters, we had planned to go to the livestock auction on Saturday, and I was just wondering if that was still on."

She tried to think what day it was, but her brain seemed to have stopped working. Still, she could trust Ty to know what to do.

"I don't know that you can count on Jack, with Mom still in the hospital. Why don't you just use your own judgment, okay?"

"Sure thing. I'll go and see if they have what we're looking for." He let his gaze stray toward Maddie. "Night, ma'am. Violet." He strode toward the back door, settling his Stetson squarely on his head.

"Nice to have such a good-looking cowboy around," Maddie said once the door had closed. "Is there anything special between you two?"

"Definitely not." Violet shook her head. "Ty's a great guy, but like everyone else around here, he treats me as if I'm about twelve or so. Maybe younger. He seemed to appreciate you, though."

"Please." Maddie shuddered. "I'm through with men. One broken engagement was enough for me." She picked up her cup and started toward the living room.

The front door burst open. Jack came through, as brash as ever. He tossed his hat in the direction of the hook on the credenza, catching it perfectly. He caught sight of Maddie first, as she stood directly under the hall light.

"Hey, Vi, where did you disappear to—" He stopped. Blinked. And looked past Maddie to where Violet stood. And looked again. "What is going on here?"

"Jack, this is Maddie Wallace." Violet went and stood next to Maddie, letting him compare them one against the other. "My twin."

Jack stared. With a pang, she noted the lines of strain around his light brown eyes and bracketing his firm mouth. He was taking his mom's injury hard, blaming himself, and she feared this discovery was going to make things worse.

He shook his head. "It can't be."

"It is." Violet took his arm, feeling the muscles tense under her hand. "Come into the living room and sit down. We'll talk about it."

Unwillingly, he nodded and let himself be led to the overstuffed leather couch. He slid down into it, looking almost boneless. But the tension was still there, in the lines on his face and the tightness of his jaw.

"Okay, I'm not going to argue the point of whether or not you're twins." He stared at Maddie. "I can't. This isn't just a resemblance...you're identical. How did you find her?"

"Maddie," Maddie said, her voice tart. "My name is Maddie, and like it or not, I'm your sister."

Jack looked taken aback for an instant. Then he managed a strained smile. "Sorry, Maddie." He shook his head, looking as if he'd taken a fall. "What does this mean? Vi, if you have a twin we've never even heard of, then maybe nothing we think we know about our past is true. What if I'm not really your brother?"

"You are. I know that." Violet clasped his hand, her heart hurting for him. "Maddie, show him the photo."

Maddie got out the framed picture she'd brought along and handed it to Jack. He stared for a long moment at the face that was the image of his own.

He put the picture down carefully, lunged from the couch, and strode across the room, looking as if it weren't big enough for him. Violet recognized the signs. When he was hurting, Jack had to be alone. Usually he'd take one of the horses and ride until they were both exhausted.

"Jack..." Her voice was filled with sympathy, but she didn't know how to make him feel any better about this. He'd already been struggling with guilt over the quarrel he'd had with his mom right before her accident.

He held up his hand, obviously not wanting to hear more. "Don't, Vi. I don't get it. How could Mom keep this from us all these years? I feel like my whole life is a lie. Is my name even Jack Colby?"

She didn't have an answer for that. It might be Wallace, she supposed, but they didn't even know if that was right.

"I don't know," she said carefully. "Maddie's father is away. She's trying to get in touch with him. When she does, maybe he'll have some answers."

Jack spun, facing them, his hands clenched into fists. "So you expect me just to wait while some stranger decides to tell me about my own life? I can't do that. I've got to—" He stopped, shook his head. "I've got to get away until I can clear my head."

"Jack, don't." *Don't go away and leave me to face this alone*—that was what she wanted to say.

"I have to." He was already headed for the door. "I'll take my cell phone. Call me if there's any change in Mom's condition." He yanked open the door and charged out. The door slammed behind him.

Violet fought down a sob. Her family really was breaking apart, and her efforts to smooth the waters had only made things much, much worse.

Chapter Three

Landon's mind was still on that encounter with Maddie's unexpected twin when he arrived at his office the next morning. The long arm of coincidence had really extended itself when he'd walked into that coffee shop yesterday.

Or maybe it wasn't coincidence at all. He stopped in there often, sometimes with Maddie. Maddie was there even more often alone, living as close as she did. Still, he couldn't quite see why Violet would take such a chancy way of approaching Maddie, even if she had known of her existence.

Despite his caution, he had trouble imagining that Violet was anything other than she seemed. She'd been genuinely shaken at the sight of Maddie. He didn't think she could have faked that.

Odd, that Violet could be so like Maddie in appearance and yet so different in other ways. Violet gave the impression of a woman with a warm heart combined with a strong will. Sometimes that could be a dangerous mixture.

He pushed open the door to the office, which was discreetly lettered Derringer Investments. The firm had little need of obvious advertising. Their clients came to them by word of mouth—by far the best way, as far as he was concerned.

"Good morning, Landon." Mercy Godwin, his secretary, receptionist, assistant and good right arm, was at her desk ahead of him as always. Mercy's row of African violets on the windowsill made an unexpected display of color in a place of business.

He'd agreed she could have one plant in the office, back in the mists of time when they were just starting out. Somehow the number of violets had multiplied along with their clients.

"Morning, Mercy." Sometimes he wondered how she timed her arrivals. No matter how early he walked in, she was already there.

"Your schedule is fairly clear today." She frowned at her computer screen, as if daring it to come up with an event she didn't remember. "Dave Watson called. He'll be here in about fifteen minutes."

Mercy didn't ask why the private investigator was coming in. Never displaying curiosity was one of her admirable traits. In her fifties, plump and graying, she was a childless widow whose life revolved around her work. He wasn't sure what he'd do when she decided to retire.

He'd actually contacted the private investigator before he'd left the coffee shop yesterday. The sooner his doubts about Violet Colby were put to rest, the better. Dave would start with the whole question of whether or not the twins were born in Fort Worth. Apparently he had results already.

"That'll give me time for a quick look at my email first. I took a break from business yesterday."

Taking a break in this case had meant driving out to the ranch where he boarded his horse and setting off on a long ride, followed by a late swim and an early bed, with all connection to the outside world strictly forbidden. He'd adopted the weekly ritual when he'd realized that if he didn't take a breather from the tyranny of constant communication on a regular basis, he'd burn out before he was forty.

Nodding to Mercy, Landon went on into his office. Simple and understated, it suited him. His business was almost entirely electronic, and costly decorating was unnecessary, besides not to his taste. Sinking down in his leather desk chair, he scanned quickly through his email, mentally classifying the messages in order of importance as he did so, until one name stopped him cold.

Maddie. According to the time, she must have sent the message about an hour after they'd parted the day before. He clicked on it.

I've decided to go to Grasslands with Violet for a visit. Thanks for finding her. I can take it from here.

Please forget about proposing. We both know that what we feel for each other isn't enough to build a marriage on. You only proposed out of some notion that you need to take care of me, but you don't. I'll take care of myself.

I'll call you when I get back. In the meantime, I think it's better if we're not in touch.

Landon sat frowning at the message for a long moment. Maddie had gone off with a woman she'd known for all of an hour, and she didn't say when she was coming back. He didn't like this one bit.

Maybe Maddie was right, and his relationship with her wasn't a good basis for marriage. He'd promised her brother Grayson he'd look after Maddie when all the Wallace men were away, so he'd been trying to do that.

The proposal had sprung out of sympathy and caring at a time when she'd been distraught, crying on his shoulder over the loss of her promising job and the lack of support she felt from her family. Somehow he'd thought proposing would make things better. It hadn't. That was one time when his sense of responsibility had led him astray.

Frustration tightened his nerves. Never mind his reasons. He still cared about Maddie's welfare, and she needed someone to watch over her.

She'd probably dismiss that as an old-fashioned ideal, but he'd felt that way since he'd started hanging around with her brother when they were in their teens.

The Wallace kids had lost their mother, their father was absent more than he was present, and in Landon's view, Grayson hadn't done enough to take care of his little sister.

Pain gripped Landon's heart at the thought, and he seemed to see his own sister Jessica smiling at him, looking at her big brother with so much love. His guilt, never far away, welled up. He hadn't taken care of his little sister. If he had, she'd never have gotten into a car with a drunken teenager, never been in the crash, never ended her life far too soon. Maybe that was why he felt such a need to look after Maddie.

A tap on the door interrupted the memories before they could cut too deeply. He looked up with a wave of relief. "Come in."

Dave Watson lounged into the room, deceptively casual in jeans, a T-shirt and a ball cap. He managed to look like a good old boy interested in nothing more than the Cowboys' prospects for the upcoming season. In actuality, Dave was as shrewd as they came and in Landon's opinion, the best investigator in Fort Worth.

"Hey, chief. How's it going?" Dave wandered across the room and slumped into the visitor's chair.

"You tell me." Landon studied the private investigator's face, but Dave didn't give anything away. "Do you have results already?"

Dave shrugged. "It wasn't exactly a challenge. No twin girls were born in any hospital in Fort Worth on the date you gave me."

"You're sure?"

The P.I. just looked at him in response. It had been a silly question. Dave wouldn't report unless he was sure.

So that left the question hanging. Had Violet been lying, or just ill-informed? Either way, Landon didn't like it.

He came to a quick decision. "I want you to expand the search. Same date, but take in Dallas and the surrounding area, okay?"

"Will do." Dave raised an eyebrow. "Is that all?"

"For now. I might need more later." Landon shoved back from his desk in a decisive movement. "I'm going out of town for a few days. Call my private cell number if you find anything."

Maddie might think she'd ended things between them, but she couldn't end his sense of responsibility for her. Regardless of whether Violet was on the up-and-up or not, he had a bad feeling about this situation. Either way, Maddie could end up hurt. It was his job to see that didn't happen.

"Was this the best facility to deal with her care?" Maddie asked the question as they walked through the hospital lobby in Amarillo the next morning.

"It has the highest-rated trauma center in this part of the state," Violet said. "Luckily, Jack saw the accident, so he called for help on his cell phone right away. Doc Garth was there in minutes." She'd be forever grateful for that. Without Doc's prompt care, her mom might not have made it as far as Amarillo. "As soon as the doctor realized how bad it was, he had her airlifted here."

Maddie nodded. "I didn't mean my question to sound critical. Really. I've spent most of my life in the city. The ranch seems so remote in comparison."

"I guess so. It's just home to me." She smiled as they got on the elevator. "You can't imagine how stressed I was driving in Fort Worth traffic. I can drive from the ranch clear into Grasslands without passing another car."

An older woman got into the elevator after them, doing a double take as she looked from one to the other. Violet wasn't sure how to respond. So this was a taste of what it was like, having an identical twin.

If they'd been raised together, would they have dressed alike? Would they have had their own private jokes and secrets that no one else was allowed to know? Sorrow filled her. It was strange, to be mourning the loss of something she'd never had. Did Maddie feel the same, or didn't it bother her?

The elevator doors swished open, and Violet's stomach lurched. The hospital was nice enough, as hospitals went. She led the way down the long corridor toward her mom's room. Bright, cheerful, with none of the antiseptic odors she remembered from a brief hospital stay when she was six.

Despite that, Violet's spirits were dampened each time she came through the doors. No matter how cheerful she tried to be, just in case her mom was actually hearing her, fear hung on her like a wet, smothering blanket on a hot Texas day.

"It's the next room down," she said, and tried to pin

a smile on her face when she saw the apprehension in Maddie's eyes. "It'll be all right. One of the nurses told me that coma patients can sometimes hear what's said, even if they can't respond. So she may know you're here. Know we've found each other."

"I hope so," Maddie murmured, and Violet had the sense that she was praying silently. Whispering a prayer of her own, Violet squeezed her hand and walked with her into the room.

Sunlight streamed across the high hospital bed, and machines whirred softly. Belle was motionless, lying much as she had been when Violet left yesterday. A lifetime ago, it now seemed.

"Mom?" Violet covered her mother's hand with hers. How odd it was to see Belle's hands so still—she was always in motion, and even in conversation her hands would be moving.

No response, and Violet fought to keep that fact from sending her into a downward spiral.

"One day when I say that, you're going to open your eyes and ask what I want." She kept her voice light and gestured for Maddie to come closer.

Maddie's face had paled, and tears glistened in her eyes. She seemed to be searching Belle's features, maybe looking for herself there.

"I brought someone to see you, Mom. You're going to be so surprised. It's Maddie. Can you believe that? We've found each other, after all this time." She gave her sister an encouraging smile. "Say something to her."

"I'm so glad to see you." Maddie's voice wobbled a little on the words. "I didn't know. I never guessed that my real mother was out there someplace. Not until I walked into a coffee shop in Fort Worth and saw Violet sitting there."

Violet stroked her mother's hand, willing her to hear. "We look exactly alike, Mom. Did you realize we would? I suppose we must have, even when we were babies."

The enormity of the whole crazy situation struck Violet, and suddenly she couldn't control her voice. She couldn't keep pretending that this deception was okay.

"Why, Momma?" The words came out in a choked cry, in the voice of her childhood. "Why didn't you tell us?"

But her mother didn't answer. Maybe she never would. For the first time in Violet's life she faced a problem without her mother to advise her. The loneliness seemed to sink into her very soul.

And then she felt an arm go around her. Maddie drew her close, her face wet with tears for the mother she'd never known. As they held each other and wept, Violet knew she'd been wrong. She wasn't alone.

It was late afternoon when Violet finally got to Grasslands that day. She wouldn't have bothered going to town after driving back from Amarillo, but she was responsible for the Colby Ranch Farm Stand, and she had to be sure things were going smoothly.

Maddie had opted to stay at the ranch rather than come into town with her, and Violet couldn't help feeling a bit of relief at that decision. The two of them had attracted enough second glances in Amarillo, where no one knew them. Violet could just imagine the reaction in Grasslands, where every single soul could name her. She'd have to figure out how she was going to break the news to friends and neighbors, but at the moment, it was beyond her.

She hurried into the cinder block building on Main Street that housed the farm stand. The stand had grown and changed a lot since it had been nothing more than a stall along the side of the road. She liked to think she'd had something to do with that growth.

Jack had never shown an interest in the produce fields and the pecan grove, and his only reaction when assigned to weeding or planting duty had been a prolonged moan. Belle had never listened to that, and when they were growing up, they'd both learned how to do every chore that was suitable to their ages. It had been good training for the future.

Violet had never understood her brother's distaste for farming. From the time she could trot after Ricardo, Lupita's husband, she'd gone up and down the rows with him, learning where the soybeans grew best and which types of tomatoes to plant. She'd never been happier than when she had her hands in the dirt.

She took a glance at her short, unpolished nails as she pushed the door open and grimaced. That was certainly one way folks could tell her apart from Maddie, whose perfectly shaped nails were a deep shade of pink.

Violet stepped into the large, cool room that formed the main part of the building, with storage facilities and refrigerated lockers in the back room. This place was home to her, just as the ranch was. It might not be fancy, but it was the product of her hard work and vision.

"Violet!" The exclamation came before she was a step past the door, and Harriet Porter came rushing to give her a vigorous hug.

Harriet, tall and raw-boned, admitted to being over sixty, and most folks thought she was pretty far over, but age didn't slow her down a bit. She could manage the farm stand with one hand tied behind her back.

"Honey, I'm so glad to see you. How's your momma? Is there any change?"

Violet had to blink back a tear at the warmth of the welcome. "Not much change, I'm afraid. The doctors say she's stable, but..." She lifted her hands in a helpless gesture, not knowing any more positive way to say it.

"I'm sure sorry about that." Harriet gripped her arm. "Belle's a fighter, though. Don't you forget. She'll come out of this, you'll see."

Violet could only nod, because her throat was too tight for anything else.

"Mind, now." Harriet shook her finger at Violet. "Don't you let it get you down, y'hear? We grow strong women in Texas, and your momma is one of the best. I reckon the good Lord knows how much we need her here."

Not as much as Violet needed her, but that went without saying.

"How have things been going? I'm sorry I haven't checked in with you more often."

"Honey, don't you think a thing about it. You know I can deal with the stand for as long as you need. And the kids are doing fine."

Harriet had a revolving procession of local teenagers who worked for the stand, carting produce and stocking bins. Harriet always referred to them collectively as "the kids," but she took an interest in each one. They'd get the rough side of her tongue in a hurry if they didn't pull their weight, but she was a staunch defender when any of them needed help.

"That's good." Violet was already sending an assessing gaze around the interior. It was nothing fancy, that was for sure, with concrete floors and cinder-block walls, the produce stacked on long tables or in bins. It was spotless as ever, but Violet noticed a few empty spaces on the tables. "No sweet corn?"

Harriet's gaze grew dark. "That Tom Sandy tried to palm off corn that must have been picked two days ago on us. I told him what he could do with his stale corn. Why, the sugar would all be turned to starch in it by then. I'd rather do without than put that out. Our customers expect the best."

True, but it really would be better if Harriet didn't antagonize one of their suppliers. That had been a change Violet had implemented, buying from some other growers instead of selling only their own produce. It gave them a wider assortment of stock, but managing those growers was time-consuming, and it was a job only Violet could do.

"I'll talk to Tom," she promised. "Is anybody else giving you any problems?"

Harriet shook her head. "We sure could use more tomatoes, though. Folks keep asking, but with the weather, there just aren't enough to be had."

The weather was a constant worry. This year they'd had too much rain in the early spring, making it hard to get the plants in, followed by a prolonged hot, dry spell that had turned the soil to stone. The plants were looking better now, though, so they'd have plenty before long, she hoped.

"I'll make some calls," she said. "Try and find somebody who has them ripening now."

"Just do it when you have time." Harriet patted her arm. "I know it's rough, running back and forth to Amarillo every day. At least you have Jack to help you."

Violet managed a noncommittal smile at the reference to her brother. If he had any sense, Jack would get himself back here before folks noticed he was gone.

She was saved the task of responding by the approach of Jeb Miller. Despite Jeb's youth, he'd won the hearts of most of Grasslands in the five years he'd been pastor at Grasslands Christian Church.

"Violet." He grasped her hands in both of his. "I'm so glad to see you. I must have missed you when I went to the hospital yesterday."

"Yes, I…I had some things I had to take care of." Thankfully, Harriet had retired from earshot, probably thinking to give Violet some private time with her pastor, or she'd have been asking where Violet had been.

"I was sorry to see there was no change." With his red hair, freckles and youthful grin Jeb might not be the classic image of a minister, but he had a warm voice that matched his warm heart. "I prayed with Belle, and I trust she was able to hear and be comforted."

"Thanks, Jeb. I don't know what we'd do without you."

He shrugged, as if to dismiss the need for thanks. "Folks have been wanting to bring food out to the house, but Lupita keeps saying that's not needed. I hope you know your whole church family stands ready to do anything that will help. The prayer chain is going strong."

"I'll let you know if anything else comes up." It was on the tip of her tongue to confide in Jeb about Maddie, but she restrained herself. That was a conversation better held in the privacy of the reverend's office.

"Now, I'm sure you haven't had a minute to think about Teen Scene staffing for this weekend—"

"Oh, my goodness." She stared at Jeb in consternation. "I'm afraid it went clear out of my mind."

Surprising, since the Teen Scene program was her baby. An effort to provide Grasslands' teens with a wholesome alternative for entertainment on Friday and Saturday nights, it made use of the church gym and adjoining lounges for activities. One of her challenges was to keep it staffed with adults she could count on.

"I'm sorry I forgot about it. I'll get right on it—"

"No need for that." Jeb grinned, shoving his horn-rimmed glasses up on his nose. "It's already done. And don't you think about coming back until life settles down a bit. We'll muddle along, I promise."

"I'm so grateful." There were the tears again, threatening to break loose. "It won't be long."

"Well, don't worry about it." He glanced over her shoulder toward the racks. "I need to pick up a few things, and then I'd best drop in the office again and catch up on paperwork. I'll be interviewing people for the secretary's position tomorrow, and it scares me half to death."

"You'll do fine. Anyway, you know what you'd tell anybody else, God has the right person picked out already. You just have to identify her."

As Jeb grinned and moved away, Violet took another look around. Everything seemed to be going all right, other than the stocking problem. And she could make those calls from home, or in person, when it came to Tom Sandy. Waving to Harriet, she headed toward the door.

Outside, she paused for a moment to adjust her hat to shield her eyes from the sun, whose rays still shimmered from the concrete. She took a step toward her car and stopped.

She must have started to hallucinate. Either that or it really was Landon Derringer, Maddie's almost-fiancé, walking down Grasslands' main street, coming straight toward her.

Chapter Four

Violet stiffened, remembering Maddie's short description of her relationship with Landon. What was Maddie going to think when she realized the determined CEO had followed her here? There surely couldn't be another reason why a man like Landon was in a place like Grasslands.

"Violet." He touched his hat brim in greeting. "We seem to make a habit of running into each other."

"In very unlikely places." She managed a smile. "You don't seem to have any difficulty today in telling us apart."

A faint smile touched his wintry green eyes. "I should have realized you weren't Maddie at first sight yesterday. The hair is different, of course, and the clothes."

"Of course." She was a country bumpkin, in other words, in comparison to her glamorous twin.

He lifted an eyebrow. "That wasn't an insult, Violet." He seemed to have no trouble in divining her thoughts. "I like the way you look…sort of casual and windblown."

"More like hot and dusty at the moment," she said briskly. What did she care what Landon thought of her appearance? "What brings you to Grasslands?"

"I'd think that would be fairly obvious," he said.

Clearly the man enjoyed sparring with her, but she wasn't falling for it. Especially since she had much more important things on her mind. Odd, how much more confident she felt facing him today than she had yesterday. She was on her own turf now, and he was the outsider here.

"Does Maddie know you're coming?"

A faint frown line creased his forehead. "Not exactly. I was going to call her, but then I decided it was better just to come." He nodded toward the store. "When I saw the sign with the Colby name, I figured this was a good place to ask for directions. Does your family run this place?"

"Not exactly," she said, echoing his words. "The family owns it. I run it."

"You?" His surprise wasn't very flattering.

She tilted her head back to look up at him. "You know, Landon, I'm beginning to understand why Maddie broke up with you. If you're hoping to win her back, you might want to try being a little less condescending."

She had the pleasure of seeing Landon speechless for a moment. Then he grinned appreciatively.

"Score one for you. I apologize, Ms. Colby. I didn't mean to imply anything about your capabilities by my remark. Will you forgive me?"

She felt herself weakening. He certainly got a lot of mileage out of that smile, and he probably knew it. "You're forgiven. Just don't make the same mistake with Maddie."

"I'll try not to." He studied the sign over the door. "I don't think you actually mentioned the Colby Ranch yesterday. Is it a truck farming operation?"

"Don't let my brother hear you say that. As far as he's

concerned, it's a cattle ranch, and the truck farming is just a sideline."

"It must be quite a sideline to warrant a store that size." Landon nodded to the building, coming a step closer to her in the process.

"We do all right." She shouldn't let herself be pleased that he sounded impressed.

She was beginning to feel a bit confused. Landon surely was here to see Maddie, wasn't he? So why was he spending all this time chatting with her? He was leaning against the building as if he had all the time in the world.

"Something wrong?" he asked, apparently a little uncomfortable at her scrutiny.

"Not wrong, exactly. Just wondering why you're here. What do you want in Grasslands?"

"Did you expect me to let Maddie just wander off with her newly discovered twin and do nothing about it?"

Those green eyes of his could have a dangerous glint in them, she discovered.

"According to Maddie, you two are not engaged any longer. I'm not sure that her actions are any of your concern."

If he'd seemed relaxed a moment ago, all that was gone now. He frowned at her, and tension seemed to vibrate in the air between them.

"I've known Maddie since she was still a kid," he said. "Even if we aren't engaged any longer, that doesn't mean I can turn off caring what happens to her."

He sounded honest enough, and Violet found herself warming to him. Still, she owed him honesty in return, and she didn't think he'd want to hear it.

"If you really care about Maddie, I admire that," she said. "But I'm not going to do anything to upset her, either. She's had a hard enough day, seeing her mother for the first time in a hospital bed. I won't do anything to hurt her, like showing up with you in tow if she doesn't want to see you."

"You're feeling a bond already, aren't you? That twin thing people talk about."

She couldn't tell if he approved or disapproved. "We're still just getting used to the idea," she said shortly. "The point is that unless there's some good reason for your being here, I don't think you should pursue Maddie if she doesn't want to see you."

His eyebrows had lifted a bit at her tone. Maybe he was surprised at her quick partisanship, but Maddie was her sister, after all.

"What about if I have results from the hospitals in Fort Worth? Don't you think she'd want to hear about that?"

"You've found something out already?" She could feel the energy bubbling in her, ready to burst out. "How did you do that? I thought those records would be sealed. I wasn't sure the hospital records office would even let me look."

"It helps to have a good private investigator on the payroll," Landon said. "I put him on the job right after we spoke yesterday."

"Did he…is there…?" She was almost afraid to ask, for fear of being disappointed. She shook her head. "I shouldn't ask. You want to tell Maddie first, of course."

Landon must have been able to read her emotions pretty easily. His face gentled with sympathy, and he reached out to touch her hand. "I wouldn't tease you with information like that, Violet. I don't play games."

Her skin seemed to be warming where he touched, and she found it disconcerting. She moved back slightly, putting a bit more space between them. "What did you learn, then?"

"The investigator found out that no identical twin girls were born at any hospital in Fort Worth on your birthday."

"Oh." She felt herself sag with the disappointment of it. "I guess there aren't going to be any easy answers, then."

"I'm not giving up that quickly." Determination filled Landon's voice. "I've told him to check Dallas hospitals, too, and extend the search to surrounding communities. It's possible that your mother mentioned Fort Worth but it's actually one of the outlying areas. And Maddie—" He stopped as an idea seemed to hit him. "That was dumb. I never thought to ask Maddie if she knows what hospital she was born in. How stupid could I be? I guess I was so bowled over by seeing you that my brain stopped working."

"I hadn't thought of that, either." She rubbed the nape of her neck, trying to ease the tension. "Honestly, if we're going to figure this out, we're going to have to think it through. So far I've just been reacting."

"There's a lot more emotion involved for you than there is for me," he said. "But you're right. We ought to talk it over and work out the options to investigate."

She drew back a little more. "I wasn't actually including you in that *we,* Landon."

"Right." He sounded rueful. "You were talking about yourself and Maddie. But I'm not going to stop trying to help, so doesn't it make sense to pool our resources and work together?"

"It makes sense when you put it that way, but I'm not sure Maddie will agree."

"Well, suppose you take me to her, and we'll ask her?" There was that smile again. It almost broke through her common sense. Almost, but not quite.

"I'll take you out to the ranch," she said slowly. "But only if I have your word that you'll leave without argument if Maddie says so."

"Agreed," he said promptly. "My car is right across the street. I'll follow you."

Violet nodded, taking out her car keys. It made sense. She just hoped she was doing the right thing.

Landon hopped into his car and pulled onto the road behind Violet, not wanting to give her time to change her mind. But she didn't seem to be having second thoughts, and soon they were out of Grasslands and on their way to the ranch.

Not that it took very long to get through Grasslands. The town was about what he had expected: a small community with shops and businesses catering to the residents of the surrounding farms and ranches.

Acres of grassland stretched out on either side of the two-lane blacktop road, with low hills in the distancc under the huge blue bowl of the sky. The few houses were built well back from the road. Pretty country, the sort of place he'd think would bore Maddie stiff in a day or two at most, if not for the novelty of having discovered her twin.

Thanks to him. What would have happened if he hadn't walked into the coffee shop at just that time? Or if, having seen Violet, he'd gone quietly on his way and never mentioned it to Maddie?

He couldn't have, naturally. But the results were, in a sense, his responsibility, so he couldn't just walk away from the situation.

Each minute he spent with Violet went a long way toward dispelling whatever suspicion he'd entertained as to her motives. Too bad it also had such an unsettling effect on her emotions. Still, even if she were being completely honest, somebody hadn't been. Somebody had split up those children, and finding out who and why might lead to heartache.

What if Maddie ended up devastated by what she learned? It would be his fault for bringing Maddie and Violet together in the first place.

Ahead of him, Violet's right-turn signal blinked. She slowed down and turned on a gravel road that led through impressive stone gates and under an arched sign with three intertwined *C*s. This, obviously, was the Colby place.

The gravel road stretched, straight as a ruler, between barbed-wire fences along pastureland on either side. It ran about half a mile, he'd guess, before ending at a two-story brick house. Good-sized, the house had a porch across the front and what seemed to be wings going back on two sides. Outbuildings scattered behind it like so many Monopoly houses dropped on the land.

Violet pulled up on the gravel sweep in front of the house, and he drew his car in behind her. A fine layer of dust from the lane settled immediately on his hood.

He got out, wondering if Violet had taken the lane at that pace deliberately to mar the glossy finish of his car. But she was waiting for him, and she didn't seem antagonistic. In fact, she looked at him with a question in her eyes.

"I was wondering—I assume you know Maddie's father and her brothers?"

He nodded, jingling his keys in his hand for a moment before slipping them into his pocket. "I can't say I know her father very well, but I do know him. A doctor, busy as most doctors are, I guess. Grayson and I are the same age, and we've always been good friends. Carter was just a kid then, tagging along, but he's grown into quite a guy."

A question in those chocolate-colored eyes deepened. "Have you talked to either Grayson or Carter about all this?"

He shook his head. "Grayson's a cop, and he's on an undercover operation right now, which makes it virtually impossible to contact him. And Carter's in the military overseas. Hasn't Maddie talked about them?"

"Not much." She went through a wrought-iron gate, started toward the porch and he fell into step with her. "I'm not just being curious. Maddie sent an email to her dad, but he hasn't answered. She doesn't seem interested in contacting her brothers, but I thought maybe they should know about all this."

He frowned, thinking about it. "Maybe she feels she should tell her father first. And since neither Grayson nor Carter can do anything about it right now, maybe she's right about that."

"She really is alone, then," Violet said softly, her eyes shadowed.

"Are you worried about Maddie?" he asked, trying to get a sense of what was behind the comment.

"I can't help but feel responsible." She paused, her hand on the handle of the heavy-looking front door. "If I hadn't started off half-cocked looking for my father, I wouldn't have found Maddie. So if we end up getting hurt by what we find, I'm responsible."

He couldn't quite suppress a smile. "Oddly enough, I was just saying that very thing to myself—that I brought you two together, so if it goes badly, it's my fault."

She smiled back, somewhat ruefully. "Guilt trips. Maybe we should stop overanalyzing things. My mother always says if God puts you in a situation, it's for a reason."

"It sounds like your mother is a wise woman. Suppose we move ahead and find out what that reason is?"

Violet nodded, opened the door, and led the way into the Colby house.

The front door opened into a wide hallway, floored in a white tile that gave it a spacious look. The center hall led back to glass doors opening onto a patio area, where he could see pots and hanging baskets of flowers. He'd been right about the wings. They formed the sides of the patio, turning it into an enclosed courtyard, open at the back.

"This way." Violet nodded toward an archway on their left and led the way into a comfortable-looking living room.

Maddie was curled into an overstuffed chair in the corner, seeming relaxed and at ease, a photo album open on her lap. She glanced up, saw him, and all relaxation vanished. She swung her feet to the floor and stood, looking distinctly unwelcoming.

"Didn't you get my email, Landon?" Her tone was sharp. "I thought I was clear that I didn't want to see you just now."

Before he could speak, Violet crossed the room to her sister.

"Don't be mad that I brought him," she said softly. "I found him in Grasslands, looking for you."

"Well, he shouldn't have been." Maddie's eyes snapped, but at him, not her sister. "I told him there's no point in proposing again, and I'm not going to let him push me into getting married."

"I don't think he'd do that." Violet's voice was coaxing, but with a note of confidence that had been missing the day before. This was her place, of course, and that made a difference.

"Violet's right," he said, giving Maddie a rueful smile. "And you were right, too. We don't have a good basis for marriage, and I'll never mention it again, I promise."

He felt a sense of relief that the words were out in the open. Maddie had always been like a little sister to him, and he loved her that way, but marriage between them would have been a disaster.

Still, he'd made other promises—to Grayson, that he'd look after Maddie. To himself, that he'd never repeat the mistake he'd made with his own sister. He wasn't released from his need to take care of Maddie, especially when he was the one who'd inadvertently led her to this other family of hers.

"Landon has something to tell you," Violet said. "Something his private investigator found out. He promised that if you don't want to hear him, he'll leave right away."

Maddie looked at him for a long moment. Finally, she nodded. "All right, Landon. Sorry if I was rude."

"It's okay." He glanced around. "Mind if I sit down?"

"Please." As if reminded of her responsibility, Violet turned into a hostess, plumping the woven Indian design pillows on the couch and gesturing for him to sit. When he did, she perched on the sofa at the far end, as if careful not to align herself with him against her twin.

"I put my private investigator onto finding out about the hospitals," Landon said. "He has better access than you or I could hope to have. Unfortunately he came up empty. No Fort Worth hospital has a record of twin girl births on your birthdate."

Maddie looked a bit shaken at that news. She'd probably been praying for a quick answer to the puzzle. He swept on, telling her of the instructions he'd given Dave to widen the search.

"There are other things he can try," he concluded. "State birth records and newspaper files, for example. It would help if you know where your parents said you were born."

Maddie's forehead puckered. "Dad never spoke of it that I can remember. As for Mom—" She hesitated, maybe reflecting on the fact that the woman she'd called Mom hadn't actually been that. "Well, you know she died in a car accident when I was still small. I'm sure she told me I was born in Fort Worth, but I don't think I've ever known which hospital."

"Your birth certificate doesn't say?" He pursued the question, thinking he should have mentioned checking that first thing, not that she'd given him the opportunity.

Maddie looked stricken. "I can't believe I didn't think to get it out yesterday. But I don't remember that it mentions the hospital. The birth certificate certainly doesn't say anything about a twin."

He turned to Violet. "What about yours?"

"I haven't seen it in years. Not since I was filling out college applications, I don't think." Violet pushed a strand of hair behind her ear, tugging on it a bit as if that would help her think.

"Can you get it out now?" It would be interesting to see who Belle Colby had listed as the father of her child.

But Violet was already shaking her head. "It's in the safe deposit box at the bank, and Mom's the only one who has access. We're hitting a lot of dead ends, aren't we?"

"Your mother didn't put you or your brother on the access list?" His tone sharpened. That sounded as if Belle Colby had something to hide. Otherwise, she'd probably have changed that access, which was certainly the practical thing to do. How could she know that her daughter wouldn't need her birth certificate some time when she wasn't available?

"I guess it would have made sense to give one of us the ability to get in the box. She probably just didn't think of it." Violet didn't look convinced of her own words.

Maddie stirred restlessly. "There must be some way to get around this. With Violet's mother—our mother—in a coma, the bank ought to be a little flexible."

"It's a question of state law, not the bank's choice," he replied. The subject had come up a time or two in the course of his business, when a client couldn't get access to financial documents because his or her partner was incapacitated. "You'd have to go to court and show need, as well as a reasonable expectation that the person holding the box would never be able to—"

He stopped, realizing that his passion for exactitude had led him onto dangerous ground. Violet looked distraught.

"Anyway, it's time-consuming and not very practical right now," he concluded hastily.

"I should talk to Grayson, I guess," Maddie said, with an air of wanting to get off the painful subject quickly. "The trouble is that he told me not to try and contact him until he finished up a job he's on." She turned to Violet. "Grayson's a detective, did I tell you that?"

Violet shook her head. "No, but Landon mentioned it."

"He did, did he?" Maddie's expression spoke volumes of what she thought about him talking to her sister about her.

Violet seemed to realize she'd said the wrong thing. She picked up a framed photo from the end table and handed it to him.

"That's my brother. Jack."

He studied the face and gave a low whistle under his breath. It was Grayson's face, staring out at him. "You didn't tell me your brothers were identical as well."

"We didn't realize it until I went to Maddie's condo," Violet said.

"Is your brother here?" Landon glanced around, half-expecting a replica of Grayson to walk through the arch.

"He's...he's away for a few days." Lines of strain deepened around Violet's eyes. "Anyway, I guess if you're going to help us, you need to know what we do." She glanced at Maddie and then looked quickly away. "I mean, you'll need to pass the information on to the investigator."

There were way too many crosscurrents of emotion loose in the room right now: Maddie's annoyance at him for butting in, which was at war with his need to keep her safe, the efforts of both women to adjust to knowing that everything they thought they knew about their parentage was a lie, whatever was going on between Violet and her brother, even his own feelings about Violet, ping-ponging between suspicion and...

And what? He'd almost said attraction, but that was ridiculous. He hardly knew her.

"I'll pay the private investigator," Maddie announced, a challenge in her voice.

"Fine," he said, avoiding a fight. "I'll have him send the bill—"

He cut off at a step from the hallway. The woman who paused in the archway was middle-aged, Hispanic, with graying hair and a gaze that went unerringly to Violet.

"You should have told me we have a guest," she scolded gently. "No matter...there is plenty. I will put on another plate."

"You don't need—" he began, and stopped when Violet went to put her arm around the woman.

"Lupita, this is Landon Derringer, a…friend of Maddie's. Landon, I'd like you to meet Lupita Ramirez. She runs the house. And us." Violet gave the woman a loving smile.

"It's a pleasure to meet you, Mrs. Ramirez." He crossed to the hallway. "I'm sure you have your hands full. I can get something to eat in town."

She looked offended. "It would be a sad day when the Colby Ranch table could not accommodate a guest. Supper in five minutes."

She hustled back into the hall, presumably toward the kitchen. Violet glanced up at him and smiled.

"You have to stay, you know, or we'll never hear the end of it."

"I guess we can't let that happen." He looked into her face, caught by the warmth that emanated from her, as welcome as a wood fire on a cold winter day.

Whoa, back up, he reminded himself. *You just broke up with her sister.* Oddly enough, that didn't seem to make a bit of difference.

Chapter Five

Violet pushed the pillow up against the headboard of her bed, trying to get more comfortable. Her vision blurred as she tried to concentrate on the laptop screen, and she'd begun to think she couldn't answer one more message of sympathy. So many people were worried about her mom, so many were praying for her recovery. Surely God was listening to all those petitions.

Sighing, she set the laptop aside and rubbed her eyes. Landon had left soon after supper, saying he'd be in touch after he'd spoken to the private investigator again. She'd tried to give him an opportunity to speak to Maddie without her hanging around, but her twin had been quite determined not to let that happen. Apparently, Maddie really was serious about not picking up their romance again.

The more Violet saw of Landon, the more she thought he was right for Maddie, but Maddie just didn't see it that way. Violet touched her wrist, reliving the warmth that had swept through her when Landon touched her. She hadn't had that instant response to a man in...well, ever. The guys she'd dated in college had been boys in comparison, and since she'd come home to run the produce business, romance hadn't been in the picture.

She smiled, thinking of Jack's reactions when she'd turned down one of his buddies who'd asked her out.

"You're too fussy," he'd said. "You want to end up alone? It's time you were getting serious about someone."

She'd just grinned. "You're two years older than I am, remember? I'll get serious when you do."

That had ended it, as far as Jack's marital advice was concerned. But Landon—

She cut that thought off before it could go anywhere. Landon was totally unsuitable for her in too many ways to count. She wasn't going to think about him anymore.

Rolling off the bed, Violet shoved her feet into slippers. She'd go downstairs and get a snack. Then maybe she'd have enough energy to answer a few more emails.

The upstairs was quiet. Maddie's door was closed, and no light shone beneath the crack. Her sister must have gone to sleep already.

Moving quietly, Violet went down the stairs. The light in the first-floor hall was always left on, and she found it reassuring as she tiptoed down. The house was empty without her mom, no matter how many people were here.

When she reached the hallway and headed back toward the kitchen, Violet realized she'd been wrong. The television was on in the den at the back of the house. Maddie was curled up in a corner of the saggy, comfortable old sofa, watching the news.

"Hi."

Maddie jerked, turning. "Violet, you scared me! I didn't hear you coming."

"Sorry." She held up one foot. "Slippers don't make enough noise, I guess. I thought you were asleep already."

Maddie shook her head, curling her feet under her. "I never go to bed this early, no matter how tired I am. What about you?"

"I'm usually asleep by ten. I get up early so I can do the outside work before it's too hot." She gestured toward the kitchen. "I was going to get a snack. Do you want something?"

"What are you offering?" Maddie wrinkled her nose. "I know I shouldn't, after that meal Lupita fixed, but something sweet would taste good."

"It probably sounds silly in the middle of July, but I love a cup of hot chocolate in the evening," Violet confessed.

"Me, too." Maddie smiled. "Maybe it's a twin thing."

"Maybe so." She waved her hand when Maddie started to get up. "Stay put. It won't take a minute to fix, and we might as well have it in here where it's comfortable."

It was more than a minute, but not much. Violet put the mugs of cocoa on a tray along with a plate of homemade oatmeal cookies and swiped a paper towel over an errant splash of cocoa on the quartz counter that Lupita kept gleaming.

Maddie still sat in the same position when Violet went back into the den. She put the tray down on the coffee table and sat down on the couch.

Maddie sipped cautiously at the steaming cocoa. "Mmmm, perfect."

Violet leaned back, smiling. It was nice to find they had something in common, despite their different upbringings.

"You and your mother seem to be very close," Maddie said, frowning down at the mug she held. "Was it always like that between you?"

"Pretty much," Violet said cautiously, not wanting

anything she said to hurt Maddie. "You can talk about her as *our* mother, you know."

Maddie nodded. "I know. Sometimes it comes out so easily, and other times it just seems to get stuck. Crazy, isn't it?"

"That's how I feel about our father, so if you're crazy, I am, too. The normal rules don't seem to apply when you find out something that changes everything you think about who you are."

Maddie's expression was sober, but she reached out to touch Violet's hand. "At least we're not alone in this. Back to our mother...what kinds of things did you do together growing up? Baking cookies, that sort of thing?"

"Actually, I remember doing those kinds of things with Lupita. Mom was so busy helping Uncle James run the ranch that she was outside most of the time. I did lots of things with her, of course, learning to work the ranch. Jack, too. Mom's job was here where we lived, and we worked right along with her."

Violet's voice warmed as she thought about those times. Maybe it sounded strange in comparison to how Maddie lived, but when you grew up on a ranch or a farm, that was how things were. The whole family worked together and everyone's work had value to the family.

"What about you?" she asked. "Did you have a good relationship with your stepmother?"

Maddie's smile was a bit sad. "I didn't know Sharla wasn't my birth mother. She loved all of us a lot, and she did all the mom things." She hesitated. "I think she felt she had to do more because Dad was gone so much. Whenever we questioned it, or got mad because he wasn't there for a school play or a football game, she'd remind us that he was a doctor and sick people needed him."

"She sounds like a lovely person," Violet said gently.

"I missed her more than I can say after the accident. I was quite young when she died. Now…well, everything's so confused in my mind, but it doesn't change the fact that Sharla loved me. I can hang on to that fact."

"Do you think she knew the truth? I mean, obviously she knew that she wasn't your birth mother, but do you think she knew that you and Grayson each had a twin?"

Maddie looked startled. "I don't know. I hadn't even thought of that, but there was never any indication that she knew. If she did, she kept Dad's secret very well."

Violet picked up an oatmeal cookie and then put it back again. "Besides our parents, there's someone else out there who knows the truth, whether Sharla did or not. The person who sent you that note and the Bible."

"We really are on the same wavelength." Maddie pulled out the object that had been out of sight between her body and the arm of the couch…the Bible. It was a small Revised Standard version, with a white, soft leather cover—the sort you could buy at any bookstore. She opened it, taking out the letter.

"There was no information on the packaging as to where it came from?"

"Nothing. No return address at all, just my name and address in block printing. But you're right—the person who sent this knows all about us." Maddie shook her head. "I suppose there could be someone…some relative or close friend of our parents who knew the truth."

"True, but that doesn't account for the writer asking for forgiveness, does it? Why the implication that the person did something bad to our family? That almost sounds as if he or she was responsible for our parents splitting us up."

Violet found her head aching at the thought of what

had been done to them. On second thought, maybe it was her heart that ached.

"You can't have any more questions than I do," Maddie said. "In fact, I never did dismiss that note from my mind, even though I kept telling myself it was meant for someone else. It was just too odd. Now I know why I couldn't forget."

Violet touched the leather cover of the Bible. "Is anything written inside?"

Maddie shook her head. "I've gone through it three or four times. Nothing. And why didn't you get the Bible and note as well? I mean, if this person was responsible for splitting us up, he or she hurt you and Jack as well. Why just send it to me?"

That hadn't occurred to Violet. "I don't know. Maybe you were easier to find, for some reason."

"I guess so." Maddie was looking down, seeming to stare at the Bible. "I'm in the phone book, so anyone who knew my name and that I lived in Fort Worth could find me." She hesitated. "You could have, Violet."

Violet stared at her twin for a long moment as the meaning of her words sank in. "You think I sent the Bible? That I planned this whole thing?"

Maddie pressed her lips together. "I don't want to think that. But I can't ignore the fact that you could have."

"I could have if I'd known you even existed, but I didn't. Can't you see that I'm at as much of a loss as you are?" Violet discovered that there was something worse than all the unanswered questions. It was realizing that Maddie didn't trust her.

She started to get up, knowing that if she sat there any longer she'd start to cry. Maddie grabbed her arm.

"Violet, don't go. I do believe you. But once in a while

the doubts creep in, and I wonder if I can trust anyone. My whole life has been turned upside down."

"Mine has, too. Remember?" She wanted to be angry, but she understood what Maddie was saying. "Sometimes the doubts ambush me, too. But you're my twin. I keep coming back to that. Not trusting you would be like not trusting myself."

"I know." Maddie's voice was small. "I just felt like I had to say it, instead of letting it eat away at me. I'm sorry if I hurt you."

"It's all right." Violet managed to smile, wanting to show there were no hard feelings. But that wouldn't be true. The hurt still lingered. She had to remind herself that twin or not, it was going to take time to build a relationship between them.

Landon drove toward the ranch house the next morning, his thoughts shifting from the business that had kept him on the phone for several hours to the problem that lay ahead of him: convincing Maddie to go back to Fort Worth.

The ability to concentrate fully on the issue of the moment was one of his strengths, but it seemed to be deserting him just when he needed it most. Violet's image kept coming between him and his need to do what was best for Maddie.

How could he have mistaken Violet for Maddie, even for a moment? Now that he knew them both, he could probably identify them if he were blindfolded. Despite the external similarities, Maddie and Violet each had a distinctive personality that was all her own. Violet had a glow about her—a welcome warmth that seemed to draw him closer each time he saw her. He'd known instinctively that whoever was at fault in this tangled situation, it wasn't Violet.

And the tangle had gotten worse, judging from the call from Dave.

His fingers tightened on the wheel as he made the turn into the lane. Dave, with his customary thoroughness, had gone the extra mile in trying to find out what he'd been asked, checking birth records in Belle Colby's name as well as in Brian Wallace's. That had led him farther than even he had expected.

"Belle Colby doesn't exist," he'd said flatly.

"What are you talking about? The woman is in a hospital in Amarillo. She's real, all right." He'd been impatient, eager to get on with the business at hand.

"She may be real, but she's not Belle Colby." Dave's sureness rang in his voice. "I've checked and cross-checked. Whoever she is, she has a manufactured identity. It's a good job, but not quite good enough."

"Can you find out who she really is?" Landon had focused in on this new issue.

"I don't know." Dave would never promise what he couldn't deliver. "It's easier to find out who someone isn't than who they are, if you get my drift."

"Do your best. Put more people on it if you have to. I need to know what's going on here."

"Will do." Dave had clicked off, needing nothing more to put a full-scale search into operation.

And Landon had headed straight for the ranch. Whatever was going on, he wanted Maddie out of it. He glanced at his watch. If they'd already left to go to the hospital—but no, Violet's SUV and Maddie's compact were parked on the gravel sweep in front of the house. He pulled in behind the vehicles and got out, urgency riding him.

Violet might know nothing at all about her mother's past. But if she did, her instincts were wrong, and she'd been deceiving them. Either way, that didn't alter the fact that by staying here, Maddie was getting involved in something that was probably way over her head.

Violet pressed soil firmly around a pepper seedling that had been disturbed by something during the night. She'd have to double-check the fence to see how the unwelcome visitor had gotten in. If she—

A shadow fell across the plant. Startled, she looked up. Landon was a tall, dark outline with the sun behind him.

She stood quickly, pulling off her gloves. "Landon. I didn't expect to see you this early." Sometime in the wee hours of the night she'd formulated the words to something she wanted to tell him, but she hadn't expected to have the opportunity this early.

"I thought I'd stop by before you and Maddie headed out for Amarillo. At least, I assume you're going to see your mother today?"

There was an undertone to his words that Violet couldn't quite identify. Disapproval? But that was ridiculous. He couldn't disapprove of Maddie going to see her injured mother.

"I needed to get some work done here before it's too hot, so we'll go after lunch. Maddie is in the house if you want to see her."

He didn't move, glancing down the rows of plants. "So this is your domain, is it?"

"Part of it." She waved a hand to the other planted fields. "At the moment we have several kinds of peppers, tomatoes, okra, black-eyed peas and green beans. And the pecan groves, of course."

Following the direction she was pointing, Landon looked toward the pecan groves in the distance. "You have an impressive operation here." That sounded somewhat reluctantly admiring. "You never wanted to do anything else with your education? Teach, for instance?"

Violet shook dirt from her gloves. "Something where I wouldn't get my hands dirty, you mean?"

"Am I sounding condescending again?" Landon gave her a trace of a smile.

"Maybe just a little." She glanced at the rows of plants. "This is satisfying. Plants are predictable, unlike people. Given the right circumstances, they'll flourish."

"Speaking of which, isn't it too hot to be planting now?" he asked.

It was a more intelligent question than she'd have expected from someone who looked as if he couldn't tell the difference between an asparagus plant and a weed. "We plant peppers a couple of times a year. The plants we set out in July give us a fall harvest."

His eyebrows lifted. "You sound like an expert. Did you study horticulture?"

She couldn't help the chuckle that escaped. "Actually, I majored in English literature. I can't say that knowledge of Shakespearean sonnets improved my gardening abilities, but it has enriched my life."

Violet had surprised herself with her answer. She usually turned off that question with a joke, but somehow she'd found herself telling Landon what she really felt.

He was studying her face, his expression grave. "I see the Colby family is full of surprises."

If her cheeks had reddened, maybe he'd think it was from the sun. "Yes, well…" This was her chance to say what she'd been rehearsing, so she'd better do it. "Before you go in to see Maddie, there's something I wanted to say."

Wariness settled on his face. "Yes?"

"I know I've given you a hard time once or twice." That was probably an understatement. "But it's good of you to go to so much trouble to help us. And if you're here because you're trying to get Maddie back, I don't want to stand in your way."

Landon just stood looking at her for a long moment. Then he shook his head. "We're not engaged any longer," he said flatly. "To be honest, I think it only happened because Maddie was feeling vulnerable. She'd lost her job, and with her family away, she needed someone to turn to. And I proposed because..."

He stopped, and she didn't seem to be breathing while she waited for whatever else he was going to say.

Landon shook his head. "It's complicated. Maddie always felt like a younger sister to me. Grayson's in a dangerous line of work, and he asked me to promise to take care of her." A faint smile crossed his face. "I'm sure he didn't mean I should propose to her. I don't love Maddie that way, and she's made it abundantly clear she doesn't feel that way about me, either. I think we're both relieved to be un-engaged."

"But you're still here," she pointed out.

"With all that's happened, I expect she's still vulnerable. So I'm still keeping my promise." His gaze seemed to be probing her thoughts. "At a guess, you're probably pretty vulnerable right about now, too."

She had to shake off the sudden longing to lean on him. "Me? I'm fine. I mean, worried about Mom, of course, but otherwise, I'm okay."

Again, he paused, and she had a sense that he was censoring several things he might say. "I hope so," he said finally, and then he turned and walked toward the house.

Violet looked after him for several minutes. Then, shaking her head, she got back to work. But she couldn't quite dismiss Landon from her thoughts. He'd sounded odd…as if there was an undercurrent she couldn't reach beneath everything he said.

Well, she didn't need to understand him, she scolded herself. He was Maddie's friend, not hers.

In another fifteen minutes she'd finished with the pepper plants. There was certainly plenty to do elsewhere, but if she was going to get a shower and be ready to leave for Amarillo after lunch, she'd better get on with it.

Returning to the house, she crossed the courtyard to the back door and went in quietly, taking off her work boots in the hall.

Maddie and Landon were in the living room, judging by the murmur of voices. Hopefully she could slip up the stairs without disturbing them.

She reached the bottom of the staircase when Landon's voice rang out sharply.

"Listen to me, Maddie. You have to come back to Fort Worth with me now. These people aren't what you think."

She was frozen for an instant, unable to think, only to feel pain. She'd begun to trust Landon. She'd believed he trusted her. And all the time he'd been planning to take her sister away.

The pain surged into anger, and the anger propelled her into the living room. Maddie and Landon stood facing each other, tension in the air between them.

"What are you doing?" The words burst out of her. "I thought you were our friend. Why are you trying to take Maddie away?"

Maddie crossed the few feet between them and put her arm around Violet's waist, facing Landon with her. The gesture of solidarity warmed Violet's hurting heart.

"What *are* you doing, Landon?" Maddie asked. "You said you wanted to help me. Us."

Landon's face had grown rigid. Forbidding. "I am trying to help you." Clearly he was talking just to Maddie. "I'm not saying you have to cut off ties to Violet, but you'd be better off at home until we can sort all this out."

"You don't have the right to tell me what to do. Nobody does. I'm a grown woman, and I can make my own decisions."

After the previous night's doubts, Maddie's support touched Violet's heart. She wanted to speak, wanted to tell Landon just what she thought of his actions, but maybe this was between Landon and Maddie.

"If your father or Grayson were here, I'm sure they'd agree with me." Landon took a step toward Maddie, holding out his hand.

"They're not here, and even if they were, I wouldn't leave without a good reason." Maddie's eyes sparked with anger. "So unless you can explain yourself a little better, I think you're the one who should leave."

"You want a good reason?" Landon, apparently finding his patience stretched beyond endurance, snapped. "Fine, I'll give you one. Dave looked into the antecedents of the woman named Belle Colby, and you know what he found? He found that Belle Colby doesn't exist. So whoever is lying in that hospital bed in Amarillo, her name isn't Belle Colby. And maybe Violet already knew that." He strode past them and paused at the front door, frowning at Maddie, leaving Violet alone. "Whenever the two of you decide to listen to common sense, get in touch with me. If I'm not at the hotel in town, I'll be back in Fort Worth."

The door slammed behind him, adding an exclamation mark to his words.

Chapter Six

"Do you think it's true?" Maddie broke the silence that had stretched between her and Violet for most of the miles to the hospital as they were pulling into the parking lot.

"I don't know." Violet switched off the ignition and rubbed her temples, feeling as if her head were about to explode. "I don't think Landon was lying. But he's wrong to think I know any of this." Landon's attitude was a separate little pain in her heart.

"Landon." Maddie said the name explosively as they walked toward the hospital entrance. "I'm just plain mad at him. I've told him it's over between us. Why does he have to keep butting in?"

The hospital doors swished open and then closed behind them, giving Violet a moment to compose her thoughts.

"He still cares what happens to you," Violet said, keeping her voice mild with an effort. It was only too obvious that Landon didn't care what happened to her. That shouldn't hurt so much. She pushed the elevator button. "You've known each other for a long time. If he were in trouble, you'd want to help him, wouldn't you?"

"I suppose so," Maddie admitted. "But he's a friend, not a big brother. Or a boyfriend."

They stepped onto the elevator. "That's how Jack is," Violet said. "Always thinking he has to take care of me because he's the big brother."

Except for now, when she really needed his help.

"Jack's not being very helpful from wherever he is at the moment." Maddie's voice was tart. She darted a look at Violet. "Sorry. I know you're close to him, but honestly…"

"He's picked a bad time to go AWOL." She had to smile, although it wasn't funny. "We could use Jack, but he's not here. And you don't want Landon, but he won't go away." She wouldn't let herself think about wanting Landon.

"Men," Maddie said, a wealth of meaning in the word. The elevator doors opened and they stepped out onto their mom's floor.

There wouldn't be any change; Violet knew that. Still, she couldn't stop hoping every time she walked in the door. Today might be the day her mom woke up.

It wasn't. Violet's disappointment was mitigated a little by the fact that Maddie didn't hang back this time. She went straight to her mother's bed and pulled up a chair, bending over to touch a passive hand before she sat down.

"Hi," she said. "It's me, Maddie. Violet and I are both here with you."

"That's right, Mom." Violet bent to kiss her mother's cheek. "I think you have a little more color in your face today."

Actually their mom was ashen beneath her tan, but she had to have hope, didn't she?

Maddie rose, moving restlessly to the window.

"Landon always said that private investigator of his was the best in the business." Obviously Landon's revelations were eating at her, just as they were at Violet.

Violet moved away from the bed to join Maddie at the window. Probably, Mom couldn't hear their words anyway, but she didn't want to take the chance. She'd been thinking of little else since Landon slammed out of the house, so they may as well talk about it.

"Well, even if Mom changed her name, that's not a crime." She kept her voice down, her back to the bed. "Maybe she had a good reason. Maybe she was upset and wanted to make a fresh start." But she knew even as she said the words that they didn't make a whole lot of sense.

"If she changed her name, that means she changed yours, too." Maddie looked at her, and for a moment Violet had the dizzying sensation that she was looking in a mirror. "Did you think of that? Maybe you're really Violet Wallace."

She tried the name out mentally, not liking the idea. "I've always been a Colby. I think I'll stick with that, even if…" She paused, and then shook her head. "Mom could have changed our names legally, you know."

"True." Maddie pressed her lips together for a moment, probably in frustration. "If only she'd wake up, she could answer all of this for us. What do the doctors say about the coma?"

Violet turned to stare at her mother's face. The familiar features looked much as they always did, except for the pallor. She might just be sleeping, but she wasn't.

"At first, after the surgery, they kept her in an induced coma. The doctors said it was important to the healing process. When they started lessening the medication, they said she should start to wake up, but she didn't." Her voice choked. "There's still hope."

"Sure there is," Maddie echoed loyally. "You hear about things like that all the time. I read an article about how people sometimes wake up after months, even years, in a coma."

Months. Years. The words broke through the protective shell Violet had been cultivating for the past week. The shell had been her only defense against the fear that she might never have her mom back again, but it was suddenly too heavy to bear. She couldn't do it any longer. The tears came, flooding down her cheeks faster than she could wipe them away. She buried her face in her hands and wept.

"Violet, I'm so sorry." She felt Maddie's comforting arms go around her. "It will be all right." The soft words echoed what her mom used to say to her. "Don't worry. It will be all right."

Violet cried until it seemed she had no tears left. Finally, she moved to the chair and leaned back, exhausted. Empty.

Maddie handed her a cool, wet washcloth, and Violet pressed it to her eyes.

"Thanks," she muttered. "Sorry I fell apart."

"It's okay to cry. Don't you think I have? Sometimes you just need to."

"I guess." She sighed, mopping her eyes again. "I'd rather have answers." She looked at her mom's unresponsive face. "It's just so hard to keep being hopeful, you know? I keep praying, but then I find myself wondering if God's listening."

"Do you think..." Maddie began, and then she hesitated.

"What?" Violet looked up, blinking a little. Her eyes were sore from crying, and she probably looked a wreck, but she didn't suppose Maddie would care.

"You mentioned something about running into your pastor yesterday. I was thinking that maybe we could talk to him."

"Jeb's someone we could trust with the whole story," she said slowly. "But that would mean we'd..."

"We'd have to come out in the open about me," Maddie finished for her. "I understand. People would talk." She gave a rueful smile. "I've already figured out that Grasslands isn't like Fort Worth."

Violet clasped her hand. "You know what? I don't care how much people might talk. Let them. I think it's time I made an appearance with my twin."

Maddie rewarded her with a warmhearted smile, and Violet felt ashamed that she'd ever thought of keeping their relationship quiet. Everyone on the ranch knew, of course, but however much they might talk among themselves, they wouldn't say anything to her.

Well, so what if she had to face some awkward questions? She knew what her mom would do in that situation. She'd meet the questions with a confident smile and go her own way. It seemed as if her daughters could do the same.

"I've wanted to talk to you about Maddie, but it's all been so complicated."

Violet sat back in the comfortable, sagging rocker in Pastor Jeb's office later with a sense of relief. The story had been told, and she didn't have to worry about how it would be received. Jeb's heart was big enough to listen to almost anything, as far as she could tell. For him, judgment was always best left to God. The pastor's job was to point people to Him.

"I'm glad you told me. It really is incredible." Jeb's

gaze traveled from her face to Maddie's. "You two are identical on the outside."

"The outside?" Maddie looked taken aback.

Jeb smiled. "I don't suppose God sees folks the way we mortals do, do you? 'Man looks on the outside, but God looks on the heart,'" he quoted.

"I've been holding back, afraid to bring everything out into the open," Violet admitted. "I guess God knows that, if He knows my heart. But we've decided we can't keep this a secret any longer. We need to know the truth."

"Good." Jeb smiled. "Folks are going to talk about your long-lost twin for a while. You know how Grasslands is. But I think you'll find most of them wish you well, even if they do talk. And if anyone here knows anything that will help you, I'll pray they come out with it."

The telephone rang. Jeb reached toward the receiver but the ring cut off abruptly, followed by the low murmur of a voice in the other office. He shook his head. "I keep forgetting I have a secretary now. She must have come in while we were talking."

A hesitant tap at the door was so timid it almost sounded like a faint scratch. "Come in," Jeb called.

The door opened, and the woman who stood there peered inside hesitantly. "I'm sorry, sir, but—" She stopped, catching sight of Jeb's visitors. Her eyes widened, and she grasped the edge of the door frame.

"It's all right, Sadie, you haven't developed double vision," Jeb said. "This is Violet Colby, and her twin, Maddie Wallace. I'd like you both to meet Sadie Johnson, our new church secretary. She's new to Grasslands, as well, so I hope you'll make her feel welcome."

"It's so nice to meet you, Sadie." Violet stood, starting to hold out her hand, but Sadie had backed against the door, arms folded across her chest, grasping the dull gray cardigan she wore in spite of the heat. Small and fine-boned, she looked like a waif in her baggy, oversize clothes. Anxious green eyes stared at them from behind glasses that were too big for her face.

Violet contented herself with a warm smile of welcome instead of a handshake. She recognized the signs. Jeb was a sucker for a stray, and Sadie certainly looked lost. She only hoped the woman could type, because Jeb would never have the heart to fire anyone.

"Welcome to Grasslands," Maddie said. "I'm a newcomer, too, so I know just how it feels."

Sadie gave a slight nod, still staring at them, standing in the doorway as if mesmerized.

Jeb cleared his throat. "I think you had a message for me, Sadie."

That brought Sadie's gaze to his face. "Oh, yes, sir. Pastor. That was Mr. Watson on the phone. His mother is feeling poorly, and would you stop by."

She still stood in the doorway, as if stuck there. Jeb dealt with the situation by taking her elbow and walking her back to her desk.

"I'll have to go." He glanced at them. "You know Mavis Watson. She thinks she's dying about once a month, but…"

"But you go, anyway." Mavis Watson might well outlive all of them, but Violet knew Jeb too well to think he'd postpone a visit. "Thanks, Pastor Jeb. I'm glad we told you." Violet glanced at Maddie.

Her sister nodded. "We'll be all right. Just keep our mother in your prayers."

"All of you," Jeb corrected gently. "I'll be praying for all of you."

Once outside, Maddie and Violet parted to run a few errands, agreeing to meet back at the car in half an hour.

Violet turned right and walked quickly toward Grasslands' only hotel. She'd leave it to Maddie to make peace with Landon or not, as she chose.

But talking to Jeb had cleared her mind. She might not like Landon's attitude or even his motives, but if he really wanted to learn the truth, she could hardly fault him for that. After all, she wanted answers as well. Maybe, if she caught him in a good mood, they could even sit down and have a rational discussion about his private investigator's findings.

She crossed the street, but before she reached the hotel, she realized she wouldn't have to go in and ask for Landon. He was jogging down the trail that led through the park.

Landon had told himself that a good workout was what he needed to brush the cobwebs away and let him focus. But after a few circuits of the jogging trail in the park, he knew what was bothering him had nothing to do with mental fog and everything to do with guilt.

Guilt had been a constant companion for years now, sometimes going into hiding, only to jump out at him when something reminded him of his little sister. Maddie had pushed those buttons when she'd leaned on him, all upset over what her future was going to be after she'd lost her job. And in that case, guilt had pushed him into exactly the wrong path. He didn't want to marry Maddie any more than she wanted to marry him.

He dropped to an easy jog, letting his pulse rate slow. He shouldn't have blown up at Maddie and Violet that way. Losing his temper wasn't the right method for handling anything.

Individually Maddie and Violet each had an odd effect on him. But both of them together seemed to magnify his feelings of guilt and responsibility—to say nothing of the unsettling attraction Violet held for him. It was Maddie he'd promised to protect. So why was it Violet he wanted to put his arms around?

Slowing to a walk, he headed for the bench where he'd left his towel and discovered Violet was there, apparently waiting for him.

He stopped in front of her, picking up the towel to run it over the back of his neck. Violet had the advantage over him this time—she looked cool and collected, while he was red, perspiring and out of breath, to say nothing of feeling guilty. He had to trust his instincts, and they told him clearly that Violet had been as shocked as Maddie at the revelation about her mother.

"I'm glad to see you. It saves me going back out to the ranch to grovel and apologize. Are you still speaking to me?"

Violet smiled, some slight tension in her face easing. "I think maybe the apologies should go both ways. I know you're trying to protect Maddie. And that was quite a bombshell you dropped on us."

"It felt like a bombshell when I heard it, too." He sat on the bench next to her. "So I overreacted. Look, I'm sorry for being suspicious. You really didn't have a clue about all of this, did you?"

"Not a one." She ran her hands along her arms, as if she felt a chill in spite of the heat of the day. "So many lies—how do we even begin to untangle them?"

"I wish I had the answer to that question. The investigator won't give up, but..." He spread his hands wide.

"Honestly, sometimes I just feel so...so angry. How could our parents do this to us? And then I feel guilty for being angry, especially with my mother lying in that hospital bed."

His hand seemed to tingle with the need to touch her. He longed to pull her into his arms to comfort her, the longing so intense it was hard to resist. But he had to. This wasn't the time or place. "Sometimes it's natural to be angry. I'd guess that your parents had a good reason for what they did, but you and Maddie were still hurt. They probably never imagined a situation where you'd find each other this way."

"I guess not." Violet's hands were clasped in her lap, as if she needed something to hang on to. "Mom certainly couldn't have foreseen a situation where she'd be incapacitated. She's always been so strong and capable."

"Do you think there's anything else Maddie could do to get in touch with her father?" Landon found it hard to believe that the man, mission trip or not, could be so completely out of touch in a world of cell phones and computers.

"I don't know." Violet's troubled gaze met his. "I haven't wanted to push her. She seems sensitive where her father is concerned."

"Your father, too," he reminded her.

"I know. Or at least I guess I know." She bit her lip, as if undecided. "Landon, do you think we're right to dig into the past? What if…well, if it's better left alone?"

One part of him wanted to agree that she should leave it alone, but it was probably already too late for that. "You mean what if you find out something you'd rather not know?"

Violet nodded. "I'm glad to have found my twin. I'd never want to take that back. But it seems as if everything we learn just leads to more questions, like this business of why Mom changed her name. Sometimes

I feel as if digging into our past is like digging into a minefield," she said.

He couldn't help but smile a little. "Waiting for something to go boom? I know the feeling."

"Maybe we'd be better off not doing the digging." Violet rubbed the long, graceful slope of her neck, as if the tension had knotted the muscles there. For an instant his fingers warmed with the longing to do that for her, and he had to fight off that feeling.

"Some people are satisfied with comforting lies. I have a feeling that you're someone who'd rather know the truth."

"Maybe I'm more the ostrich-in-the-sand kind of person." She managed a faint smile. "You haven't known me very long, after all."

"Not long in terms of time," he admitted. "But it's been a pretty intense few days. You can learn a lot about a person by seeing him or her under stress."

She looked at him, as if measuring how honest he was being. Well, he deserved her doubts. He never should have tried to push Maddie into leaving or insinuated that Violet knew about her mother's secret past.

His cell phone rang before he could say anything else. It was Dave. Maybe he had more answers.

"Dave. Anything new?"

"A few more details. Can you talk?"

He glanced at Violet, but if he meant what he'd just told her, he couldn't start hiding things now. "Yes, go ahead."

"I finally got hold of copies of birth certificates for both girls."

"And?"

"Maddie Wallace's seems pretty straightforward, except for one thing."

"And that is?"

"She and Grayson were both adopted by Brian Wallace's wife when she married him. So that made the wife—whose name was Sharla—their legal mother. But she wasn't their birth mother."

"At least that fits. What about the younger brother, Carter?"

"Carter is the child of Brian and Sharla Wallace, born about a year after their marriage."

The fog was beginning to lift a bit. He glanced at Violet. She was obviously waiting. "What about Grayson and Maddie's birth mother? Were you able to find a name?"

"It took a lot of digging, but we came up with it, finally. Isabella Wallace. I couldn't find a maiden name, which would help in tracing her. Still, there's one interesting thing. Isabella. The nickname *Belle* might be from that."

"You said you found birth certificates for both of them," Landon said slowly, trying to process everything that the P.I. was divulging. "What about Violet?" He heard her suck in a breath and wished this call had come any time other than when she was there, waiting.

"Violet Colby's lists her mother as Bethany Colby and her father as Jason Colby, deceased. Her place of birth is supposed to be Fort Worth General."

Landon frowned. "That doesn't seem to fit."

"That's because Jason Colby didn't exist, either. The whole thing's a fairy tale from beginning to end. And the hospital records have been doctored, as well." Dave sounded satisfied. The tougher the case, the better he liked it.

"How would Belle Colby have been able to do that?"

As Violet had said, every answer brought more confusion, it seemed.

"Good question," Dave said. "All I can tell you is that she has a new identity, and it runs back pretty far. We're still tracing it. I assume you want us to keep going?"

"Definitely." He might, a time or two, have been tempted to wash his hands of the whole tangled mess, but he couldn't stop now. He was in way too deep.

"One interesting thing has come up in the records about Belle Colby," Dave said. "She shows up in Grasslands when Violet would have been about three or so. She took a job as a sort of housekeeper/secretary to the owner of what's now the Colby Ranch. Elderly man, name of James Crawford." He took a breath. "She and the kids apparently lived there on the ranch, and when Crawford died, he left everything to her—lock, stock and barrel."

"All right." He tried not to think about what that might say about Violet's mother. "I'll see if I can get any information on that. Meanwhile, just keep digging."

He hung up, and turned to see the questions in Violet's face. They were questions he had to answer, and once he had, he somehow had to persuade both Violet and Maddie to let him continue to help them. He'd thought he was coming here to protect Maddie, and that was a big enough job. Now he had to protect Violet, too, and that might be a tall order.

Chapter Seven

Violet walked along the rows of tomato plants, trying to concentrate on her work, not on that conversation with Landon the previous day. The information his private investigator had come up with simply managed to cloud the issue, rather than clarify it.

At least she felt as if the quarrel with Landon had ended. They'd all three overreacted, but in the long run, they wanted the same thing—the truth. Unfortunately, that seemed to be in short supply right now.

She stopped by a row of Roma tomatoes. The Romas were especially productive this year, but she always had to keep an eye on them. Too much or too little rain at the wrong time could spell disaster.

"Going to be a good harvest this year, even if it's a little late." Ricardo, Lupita's husband, rose from inspecting a plant.

With an inward qualm, Violet realized that it took him longer to get up these days. Still wiry and strong, Ricardo would not admit that, just as he would never admit needing help with anything, and his age was a closely guarded secret. He had that in common with Harriet Porter, the farm stand manager.

"It does look good. All the canners in the county will be busy making sauce and salsa." She lifted her straw hat and wiped her forehead with the back of her arm.

"Your momma—how was she yesterday?" Ricardo's dark eyes seemed to grow even darker.

Not surprising. He adored her mom, treating her like a much-loved sister instead of his employer. And she relied on him and Lupita, as well. They had been her support system when she was bringing up her kids without a father.

"No change." She pressed her lips together to keep them from trembling. "We mustn't give up hope, though."

"We will never do that," he said. He glanced toward the house. "Your sister went alone to see her this morning?"

Violet nodded. "If I'm at the hospital, I feel guilty because I'm not here. And if I'm here, I feel guilty because I'm not there. I think Maddie wanted to spend a little time alone with Mom, so she went today."

"That will be good for your sister, I think." He leaned over to pull a weed that had dared to pop up under the leaves of the tomato plant. "I have not talked to her very much, but Lupita says she is a good person. Like you, but different, too."

"We keep surprising ourselves at how alike we are in some ways, despite being raised apart." She hesitated. "I just wish I could understand. Why did they break us up that way?"

Ricardo's face, creased by all the years he'd spent in the sun, radiated sympathy. "You will know one day. Until then, you already know that your momma is a person of deep faith. She would not do anything without a strong reason."

The words reassured her. Ricardo, with the patience

and wisdom that came from dedication to growing things, had put his finger on the important aspect of the puzzling situation.

"You're right." She looked at him, her heart filled with gratitude. "I do know that about Mom, no matter how bad things look on the surface."

The sound of hooves attracted her attention and she turned to see Ty riding along the edge of the field. She waved, and when he pulled up she walked over to him.

"How are things going?" She shielded her eyes with her hand, looking up at him.

His strong-boned face seemed to tighten a little, unsettling her. If there was bad news she didn't want to hear it, as selfish as that might sound. She had enough to deal with at the moment.

"No problems," he said, his tone as laconic as ever. "Nothing I can't handle."

"Good." But was it? She had a sense of things left unsaid, but she didn't know quite how to approach it. She liked and respected Ty, but it was her mom and Jack who worked with him.

He took the decision out of her hands by touching the brim of his hat. "See you later, Violet." He rode on, leaving her unsettled.

"Ty is a good man."

Violet turned, surprised that Ricardo had come up behind her. She nodded. "He does a fine job as foreman." She waited, sensing that now Ricardo had something else to say.

"People get restless when they don't know what is going to happen," he said carefully. "It makes them worry and wonder, and they don't do their jobs so well."

She was surprised at the turn this conversation had taken. "You mean Ty?"

"No, not Ty. And not my people." He gestured toward the three or four men in the soybean field, most of them relatives of Ricardo or Lupita. "But the cowpokes… I hear them talking. Wondering what will happen to their jobs. To the ranch. Thinking maybe they should be looking out for a new place."

The blow was unexpected, and for a moment she couldn't think how to respond. The cattle part of their operation was always handled by Jack and her mom, along with Ty.

"Well, the ranch isn't going anywhere, that's for sure," she said finally. "Do you think it would help if I talked to them?"

Ricardo shook his head. "It should be Jack. Your brother must come home and take on his responsibilities."

He didn't add the obvious—that she should call him.

"He was upset." She knew her voice sounded defensive.

"You were upset as well, but you did not run away." His voice was firm. "Jack must come home," he repeated.

She'd wanted to give her brother more time—time to deal with his anger and guilt, time to realize he had to come back on his own.

"I'll think about it," she said. "I promise."

What if she called him and he refused to come back? He wouldn't do that, she assured herself hastily. Jack would come if she needed him.

Unaccountably, her thoughts strayed to someone else who hadn't left. Landon had every reason in the world to go back to Fort Worth and his business, but he hadn't. He'd stayed to help.

Landon had spent several hours on work that day, eating a take-out sandwich for lunch. His hotel room wasn't the most comfortable of surroundings, but it was cool and clean, and most important, it had the internet connections he needed. He could conduct business there as long as he had to.

Thanks to Dave, he now knew a good bit more about Maddie and Violet's parentage. In his opinion, and he knew in Dave's, it was highly likely that the Isabella who had apparently been Brian Wallace's first wife was indeed Belle Colby. But until they made that actual link, he had no proof of anything.

Still, Violet had seemed to take it for granted after she'd heard what Dave had reported. She would have talked to Maddie when she got back to the ranch. With any luck, Maddie would have forgiven him for trying to tell her what to do. Maybe.

He walked out the front door of the hotel to feel a blast of heat strong enough to make him want to retreat inside again. But something far more interesting drew him forward, because both Maddie's car and Violet's SUV were parked by the Colby farm store. Apparently Violet had come out in the open about her twin sister. How was she explaining that unexpected acquisition?

He crossed the street and approached the store. If Maddie was still angry, she'd at least have to be polite to him in a public place.

Landon stepped inside, pausing for a moment before he spotted Violet at the counter. As he moved toward her, she looked up and saw him. Her face warmed.

"Landon, hey. I thought you were probably hard at work." Her face grew suddenly more serious. "What is it? Have you found out something new?"

"No, nothing." He leaned on the counter, keeping his voice down. "I'm just appreciating the values of telecommuting. Give me a phone and an internet connection, and I can work from anywhere."

"I'm sure it's inconveniencing you, staying here," she said. "If you need to go back to Fort Worth..."

He touched her hand briefly. "I'm in this for the duration." He lowered his voice still further, not wanting anyone else to hear that admission. "Are you okay with that?"

He smiled into those deep brown eyes, hoping to see an answering smile in return. She studied him for a moment that felt as if it lasted an hour.

Finally, she nodded. "I'm glad for your help. But I can't speak for Maddie."

"I know. Is she still angry?"

Violet shrugged. "I told you. I won't answer for her."

"Right." He glanced around, looking for something that would let him continue talking to Violet and refusing to think about why that was so important. "It seems as if you're having a big day today." At least three times as many people were inside the store than he'd noticed the last time he'd glanced through the window.

"That's thanks to Maddie, although I'm not sure she's enjoying it." Violet wrinkled her nose in distaste.

"Maddie?" He was startled. "Why? What did she do?"

"She's here, that's all." Violet gave a rueful smile. "We decided it was time she made a public appearance, so when she got back from visiting our mom at the hospital this morning, she came in to work. We'll let everybody satisfy their curiosity and hopefully get over it."

"You think they will get over it?"

"No," she admitted. "I'm quite sure they won't move on that easily. We'll be the talk of the town until some more interesting topic comes along."

"How's Maddie taking it?" He'd think something like

that would send her fleeing back to Fort Worth, if anything would.

Violet refused to be drawn. She just smiled. "Go and see for yourself. She's working the back counter."

Landon walked back through rows of vegetables, piled high in glossy, colorful stacks. People were buying, he noticed, along with satisfying their curiosity. They could hardly come in and go away without a purchase. Still, he doubted that the additional income would balance the embarrassment.

He found Maddie, as Violet had said, at the cash register in the rear of the store. Several people stood at the counter. Oddly enough, when he approached, they melted away, suddenly taking an interest in sweet corn or okra. Maybe they recognized him as a stranger.

Maddie eyed him warily. "Landon. I might have known you'd show up."

"Sorry I chased away your customers." He leaned on the counter, keeping his voice low again. He wasn't eager to add to the supper-table conversation in Grasslands tonight.

"They'll be back," she said, sounding resigned. "Everyone wants to talk to me, apparently. But why are you here?"

"To apologize. I already made my amends to Violet. She was kind enough to forgive me for overreacting yesterday. I hope you'll do the same."

"She doesn't know you as well as I do," Maddie said. "She wasn't the one you were bossing around."

He might have realized this would be more difficult with Maddie. "I'm sorry I overreacted to what I found out about your mother. And I had no right trying to tell you what to do. My only excuse is that I was worried about you. I didn't want you to get hurt."

He wanted those words back as soon as they came out. Maddie was bound to resent his assumption that he ought to protect her from hurt.

To his surprise, she just looked at him as if measuring the amount of his remorse. Maybe Maddie had matured in the face of all she'd learned in the past few days.

"All right," she said finally.

That doubled his surprise. "All right?" He had a feeling there must be a catch.

She nodded. "Violet and I agreed that finding out the truth is best in the long run, even if it's painful. Believe it or not, I respect your abilities, Landon. You and your investigator can find out more than Violet and I possibly can on our own. So we accept your help."

Little Maddie really had grown up. "Thank you, Maddie. You won't mind if I hang around Grasslands for a while, then?"

She frowned at that idea. "You're not thinking of proposing again, are you?"

Her suspicious expression actually made him smile. "Maddie, believe it or not, I'm convinced. You and I were never meant to be anything more than friends, and I was wrong to propose to you. All right?"

She nodded. "And I was wrong to accept." Her smile flickered. "I'm glad to be your friend, Landon, but I'm not getting married until I find someone I can't live without. But I'm still not sure it's necessary for you to stay here while this is going on."

She wouldn't be impressed if he told her that he still felt responsible for her, so he needed another good reason to stay. "It seems to me the truth lies somewhere in Belle Colby's past, and she's spent most of her adult life here. It only makes sense to do what I can in Grasslands and help you and Violet as well."

She looked at him speculatively. "Do you really mean that?"

"Sure." What was in her mind?

"Fine, then I have a job for you."

"Hauling cartons of vegetables?" He was only half-kidding.

"Violet and I are volunteering at the youth center her church runs tonight, since the scheduled people can't make it. We need a male volunteer. That's you."

She looked at him with a smug smile, obviously sure he'd try to get out of it.

"Fine," he said. "Just tell me where and when."

Violet gave up her post at the door to another Teen Scene volunteer and walked back through the church social rooms. She felt as if she was always on the alert when the program was running. Opening the church to area teens two nights a week had been controversial, with some members of the congregation ready to pounce on any problem, no matter how slight, as a reason to shut down the program.

All seemed to be running smoothly tonight, other than the last-minute replacement of volunteers when Ted and Judy Fisher got unexpected houseguests from out of town. Maddie was in the kitchen serving popcorn, hot dogs and lemonade to the kids, who always seemed to arrive hungry. Wearing jeans and a plaid shirt of Violet's, her hair pulled back, she fit in surprisingly well. And if the kids were openly curious, it didn't seem to bother her.

Violet smiled at a noisy game of air hockey that was in progress and just missed being hit by an errant Ping-Pong ball from the ongoing, informal tournament. She liked seeing the kids being active, and the variety of activities available gave everyone a chance to shine.

The door to the gym stood open, emitting the squeak of sneakers on the hardwood floor. She walked in and stood for a moment, watching. One side of the gym had a low balcony area, where it was possible to have tables and chairs. The door to the outside was also there, where a volunteer checked kids in and out.

So this was where Landon had disappeared to. He dribbled down the court, moving with an almost effortless grace, and eluded a muscular guard. For an instant she thought he'd take the shot himself, but he passed off to an undersized kid who looked momentarily surprised and then sank the basket.

Landon bent over, hands on his knees, breathing hard. In a moment, amidst a lot of good-natured kidding about his advanced age, he came off the court.

"Not bad," she said. "You almost kept up with them."

"Are you kidding?" He braced his hands on the low wall that separated the balcony from the gym floor. "They nearly ran me into the ground. Kids that age have more energy than they know what to do with."

Violet nodded, letting her gaze wander over the kids. It was a nice mix tonight, and…

"Don't let me bore you," Landon commented.

"I'm sorry." She smiled ruefully. "Maybe I take things too seriously, but I always want to be sure everyone's feeling accepted here."

Landon nodded. "I understand that. Kids are too ready to put up walls. They like to categorize each other—this one's a nerd, that one's a jock."

"And some other terms that are a lot more derogatory," she added. "They can be mean, but I think when they are, it's usually out of their own insecurity."

He studied her face. "Is that personal experience talking?"

"Was I ever mean to anyone? Probably, although Mom came down pretty hard on that sort of talk."

"Were you ever picked on?" He tilted his head slightly, and the overhead light emphasized his strong, regular features.

"Not picked on like the stories you hear now, especially with all the cyber-bullying going on. Grasslands is a small enough community that everyone knows everyone else, so it's tough to get away with that sort of thing for long. Still, it's harder to be a teenager now than it was even ten years ago."

"Maybe so." He didn't look convinced of that statement. "I remember some nasty stuff going on when I was a teen, though. Drinking, drugs."

"That's why this program is so important," Violet went on. "Not just to give the kids something to do, but to give them adults who care about them enough to volunteer their time."

Landon was frowning slightly, and she wondered why. Maybe, in the privileged life he'd had, he'd been immune to the problems other people took for granted.

"I'd think a town the size of Grasslands could afford to have a community center to provide this sort of outlet for the kids. A professional staff would be better equipped to handle problems."

"Than my group of well-meaning volunteers?" she asked, irritation edging her nerves. Who was he to come in and criticize their efforts?

"Well, wouldn't that be better?" he asked. "If a professional can do the job, why rely on untrained people who let you down at the last minute?"

"This isn't Fort Worth," she reminded him, gritting her teeth in an effort to keep from saying something she'd regret. "Like it or not, this is the only game in town for these kids. If you don't feel you want to participate, I'm sure we can manage without you."

She started to turn away, but he stopped her with a hand on her wrist. She tried to deny the wave of warmth that flooded through her.

"I wasn't denying the need you're trying to meet, Violet." His voice was low, with an intensity that startled her. "Believe it or not, I had plenty of grief of my own when I was their age. Maybe you're right. I don't know the situation here. If I'd had someone who cared enough—" He broke off, looking past her. "Is that girl crying?"

Violet yanked her attention away from Landon to look in the direction he nodded. Sure enough, Tracey Benton was huddled in a corner, trying to keep her tears to herself. Slight and small, she bent over so that her long, dark hair swung in front of her face.

"Tracey. I'll see to her," she said, pulling her hand away from Landon's. "Thanks."

Maybe it was just as well that the interruption had occurred. She went quickly toward Tracey. She'd been getting way too wrapped up in Landon's intensity. Still, she wished Landon had finished what he was saying.

When Tracey saw her coming she tried to turn away, but Violet put her arm around the girl's shoulders and led her toward the tiny room they used for an office. It wasn't the first time she'd found tears streaking Tracey's olive skin. Maybe tonight would be the time she finally broke through to the girl.

Closing the door, she settled Tracey in the only comfortable chair and gave her a bottle of water and a handful of tissues. She pulled a folding chair up so that they were knee to knee.

"It's okay to cry," she said, remembering when Maddie had said those words to her.

"I'm okay." Sniffling a little, Tracey moved as if to get up.

Violet captured Tracey's hands in both of hers. "Tracey, I said it was okay to cry. It's also okay to talk to someone about what's wrong."

Tracey didn't speak. She freed one hand to brush a strand of glossy black hair behind her ear. Her gaze met Violet's for a moment and then flicked away.

Please, God, give me the right words. Let me help her.

"I'm your friend, Tracey. I'll listen to anything you have to say, and I won't repeat it to anyone. I'll help you any way I can."

But Tracey was pulling herself together, withdrawing once again. "I'm okay, Ms. Vi. Honest. I just…somebody said something that hurt my feelings. That's all."

Before Violet could say anything else, Tracey jumped up and fled from the room.

Violet watched her go with mixed feelings, mostly doubt. Tracey's explanation might be true. The child of a Hispanic mother and an Anglo father, Tracey probably had more trouble finding her place in the difficult world of adolescence than a lot of kids.

But she had a sense that Tracey was dealing with something more than the usual teasing.

Rubbing her forehead, Violet followed her slowly, burdened down by the weight of her failure. Maybe Landon had it right. Maybe she was kidding herself, trying to do something that ought to be handled by a professional.

Chapter Eight

"Are you going to Amarillo today?" Maddie paused in carrying her breakfast dishes to the kitchen, glancing toward Violet with concern in her face. "You look tired. Maybe you ought to stay home."

Violet smiled, trying to look a bit perkier than she felt. "I'm fine. I just didn't sleep well last night."

Maddie set the dishes back down on the table and slid into the ladder-back chair next to her. "Are you worrying about your…our mother?"

"Not exactly. I mean, I keep trying to give that fear over to the Lord, but I suppose it's always there in the back of my mind."

"What, then? Landon?" Maddie gave her a shrewd look. "I saw him talking to you last night."

"Of course I wasn't thinking about him," she said, more sharply than she'd intended. "Landon's not…well, anyway, I was thinking about one of the girls at Teen Scene last night. Tracey—pretty, about fourteen, with long, black hair?"

Maddie shrugged. "That description could fit about half the girls there."

"I guess. Anyway, I've found her upset several times,

but I haven't been able to get her to open up to me. It happened again last night, and once again, she wouldn't talk to me. It made me feel so useless. Maybe Landon's right, and—" She stopped.

"Landon, huh?" she smirked. "I might have known he'd have something to do with it. What did he say?"

"Nothing that bad. He implied that professionals could do what we're doing with the teenagers a lot better, and after my failure to get through to Tracey, I began to think that maybe it's true."

"And maybe it's not." Maddie patted her hand. "Landon might just be prejudiced because he's donated a lot of money to youth center programs over the years, all of them run by professionals. And he's a business-man—his first instinct is always to call in the profes-sionals. He's not thinking about the fact that Grasslands isn't Fort Worth."

Violet smiled, her spirits lifting at her twin's sup-port. "That's just what I told him. I didn't know about his charities, though, or I'd have been more careful what I said. I think that's admirable."

Maddie clapped her hand over her mouth for an in-stant, making a face. "Don't say anything, or he'll know I told you. He keeps things like his charities secret, and the only reason I know is because he recruited Dad to help with some kids who needed surgery."

"I won't say anything, but I don't see why..." Often wealthy people made more of a show of their philan-thropy.

"It's got something to do with his sister, I think," Maddie said, her forehead wrinkling. "Jessica was his younger sister, and she died in an accident when she was a teenager. I imagine he does it in her memory."

"That's so sad." Violet had been wrong about him

then, imagining a trouble-free, privileged life for him. She should have known better. Even in the best of circumstances, people didn't get out of their teen years unscathed, and losing a sister was a terrible loss.

"Jessica was about my age, but I didn't know her since she went to a different school. I do know that Landon was never the same after she died."

"No, I guess he wouldn't be." She wouldn't be, if she lost Jack or Maddie.

Maddie stood, gathering up the dishes. "I'll take these back to the kitchen. You never did answer my question. Why don't you stay home today and get some rest?"

"If I stayed home, I wouldn't get any rest," she said ruefully. "Saturday is always a busy day at the store, and I'd feel I had to go there if I don't go to the hospital. Anyway, since I missed visiting Mom yesterday, I don't want to miss today."

"Okay. I just need to change. How soon will you be ready?" Maddie glanced at her watch.

"Say about an hour. I still have to check in with Ty and Ricardo, and there's something I want to look for in the attic. Does that work for you?"

"Fine by me." Maddie vanished in the direction of the kitchen.

Violet headed upstairs. Sometime in the night she'd tried to comfort herself with memories of the way things used to be. She'd thought of something that might be a comfort to her mom, if she could find it.

When they were little, Belle used to snuggle Violet and Jack in a knitted throw she called the story shawl. They'd cuddle together on her bed or Jack's, the shawl around them, while Belle told them bedtime stories. She could still feel the warmth of the shawl and the music of her mom's voice lulling them to sleep.

Belle wouldn't have thrown away something that meant so much to them. The shawl was probably in a trunk in the attic, stored away with other mementos of their childhood.

If she could find it, she'd take it to the hospital with her. Nobody knew what her mom was aware of. Maybe she'd find some comfort in that shawl. Violet had a feeling she would, anyway, even if Belle didn't.

Switching on the overhead bulb, she headed up the attic stairs and emerged at the top, glancing around to orient herself. Thanks to the overhead light fixture and the windows at either end, the attic was bright enough to search for something easily. And it was clean, of course. Lupita wouldn't hear of any part of her domain not receiving a periodic cleaning, even one as little-used as the attic.

For the most part, the boxes and plastic bins were marked, thanks to Belle's passion for organization. Some of the older trunks dated to her Uncle James's parents' time, and every once in a while her mom threatened to put everyone to work sorting them, looking for items that should be donated to the county historical society. So far, Violet and Jack had managed to evade that task, mainly because they were all too busy.

Slipping around boxes marked Jack's School Projects and Violet's 4-H Awards, Violet came to the trunk she thought most likely. She knelt on the floor and lifted the curved lid, wondering if God minded a selfish prayer that she be able to find the shawl.

The first few items were of more recent origin: a doll she'd won at the county fair one year, carefully wrapped in plastic; a colorful serape Jack had brought back from a trip to Mexico; two graduation caps, one white and one black. Traditionally the boys graduating from Grasslands wore black, while the girls wore white.

She put them carefully aside, smiling at Jack's probable reaction if he realized how many mementos of his youth were preserved up here. She lifted out a patchwork quilt and there, at last, was the shawl. Someone had wrapped it in a sheet, then in plastic, to protect it.

Violet pulled the shawl free of the wrappings, eager to feel it in her hands again. The yarn was soft and worn, cushiony to the touch, and she seemed to see her own small hand clutching it tightly.

Tears stung her eyes and she blinked them back. She shouldn't wallow too much in the past in front of Maddie, reminding her again of all that she had missed with Belle. But she could give herself a few minutes to remember. She drew the shawl around her shoulders despite the heat, and felt the security it had always given her. She could use that sense of security right now.

But Maddie would be waiting, and she still had things to do before they could leave for Amarillo. She leaned forward to put the other items back into the trunk and realized that there was still something in the bottom—a flat manila envelope, faded with age.

Violet picked it up, her fingers telling her that it wasn't empty before she'd even opened it. There was just one enclosure, and she drew the item out carefully, turning it over to look at it.

Her heart seemed to stop for an instant, and she couldn't catch her breath. The photo was old and faded, its surface cracked and marred. But she could still make out the image. Belle—a much younger Belle—stood in front of a small house. She held an infant in her arms and had a toddler by the hand. It had to be her and Jack with Mom in that picture. But that wasn't what reduced her to uncontrollable tears.

A man stood next to Belle. She'd only seen Brian Wallace in photos, but his looks hadn't changed that much with age. He, too, held an infant in his arms and a toddler by the hand.

It was her family—her whole family, all together.

Landon went up the stairs at the Colby house quietly, his ears still burning from Maddie's sharp words. She'd taken him to task for what he'd said the night before, telling him in no uncertain terms what she thought of him. She'd followed up her lecture by demanding that he apologize to Violet, saying he wouldn't be welcome here if he didn't make this right.

If he hadn't been the target, he might have enjoyed seeing Maddie assert herself so thoroughly. He'd always thought Maddie needed protection, but he'd begun to feel he was the one who needed protection from her.

Well, he hadn't intended his words to hurt Violet. That was the last thing he wanted to do. Apparently, from what Maddie had said, there'd been an incident with one of the teens, presumably the one he'd seen crying. Violet felt, probably thanks to what he'd said, that she should have been able to handle it better.

He still thought the teen center should be in professional hands, but his words had been careless, criticizing when he hadn't completely understood the situation. As Violet had said, this wasn't Fort Worth, and they didn't have the city's resources.

Maddie had told him he'd find Violet in the attic. The door to the stairway stood open, so he assumed Violet was still up there. He went up quietly, caught between guilt and annoyance that he had to apologize to her once again.

It took only a quick glance to find Violet when he reached the top, and the sight rocked him back on his heels. She sat on the floor in front of an old trunk, looking down at something in her lap, and she was weeping, her slim shoulders shaking with the depth of her sobs.

His heart seemed to be twisting in his chest. Quickly, before he could think about what he should or should not do, he went and knelt next to her.

"Violet." He said her name gently, his throat thickening at her pain. "What is it? Can I help?"

She gestured toward the item in her lap, seeming unable to speak through her sobs. Taking that as an invitation, he bent over to look. It was a photo—old and faded. He had no trouble recognizing Brian Wallace, though. Clearly the photo was of Brian and Belle with all four of their children.

There were no more questions about who Brian's first wife had been. He could have Dave stop pursuing that missing link, although they still didn't know the Why.

"I'm sorry," he said softly. "You just found this?"

Violet nodded. "They…they look so young. So happy." The sobs overtook her again.

He couldn't help it. He drew her into his arms, stroking her hair. She wore it loose today, and it flowed through his hand like silk. He murmured any sort of nonsense that came into his head that he thought might be soothing.

It probably wasn't a good idea, holding her this way, but at the moment he didn't care. He dropped a light kiss on the top of her head.

"I understand," he said. "You've just had too much to bear lately, and now this. You don't have to be brave all the time, you know." He stroked her shoulders, feeling them shake with her weeping.

Violet drew back a little, sniffling as she tried to contain her tears. "I'm sorry. I didn't mean to fall apart. When I looked at the picture, I realized something." She pressed her palm to her chest. "There's always been an… an empty place in me. In my heart. Now I know what it was. It's the space where my father should have been."

His own heart seemed to be ripping apart. "I'm sorry, so sorry for what they did. It wasn't fair to you." He wanted to touch her cheek, but he held back, fearing he'd cross a line and not be able to get back.

"I can't let myself go like this. I can't. Mom and Jack always tried to take care of me. Now I have to be the strong one."

Landon felt an irrational surge of fury toward her missing brother. "You have Maddie," he said soothingly. "And me."

Violet wiped her eyes with the back of her hand. "You're kind, Landon. But you've done enough. I can't involve you in my grief."

"I think it's too late for that," he murmured, and he knew it was too late for him, as well. He caressed her cheek, and then cradled her face in his hands.

Violet's eyes widened, and her breath seemed to catch. He could feel her skin grow warm against his palms.

Unable to resist, he lowered his face to hers and kissed her. Her lips were soft and warm, and she leaned into the kiss as if it were the most natural thing in the world.

Landon's pulse thundered, and the longing to draw her more fully into his arms was so strong he could barely fight it off.

But he did…he had to. He drew back, but even as he

did so, he knew he could no longer pretend he didn't have feelings for Violet.

He brushed his fingers gently along the sweet curve of her cheek and then sat back on his heels. He couldn't seem to stop looking at her the way she was at this moment…her cheeks pink, her lips soft, her eyes a little dazed.

He cleared his throat. "Is this where I should say I'm sorry?"

She shook her head, turning away as if to hide her face. "No." She put her hand against her cheek in what seemed an instinctive gesture. "But maybe we should go downstairs and forget about what just happened."

He took her hand and helped her to rise. "We can go downstairs. As for forgetting—that's something I can't promise."

Violet felt reasonably sure her cheeks were red when they reached the living room and found Maddie curled up in the corner chair that seemed to have become her favorite. She'd already dressed for the trip to Amarillo in tan pants and a silky turquoise top. Next to her twin, Violet felt grubby and disheveled.

Maybe Maddie would assume Violet's flush was from the two flights of stairs. But from the way Maddie glanced from her to Landon, Violet doubted it.

What had she been thinking of, letting Landon kiss her that way? Worse, kissing him back? True, Maddie insisted that her relationship with Landon was over, but Maddie was angry with him right now. What happened when she got over that?

"Look what I found in the attic," she said hurriedly, before Maddie could speak.

"A shawl?" Naturally Maddie focused on the larger object Violet held.

"This." Maybe she should try to soften the impact, but she couldn't think how to do that. "I found it in the bottom of Mom's trunk."

Maddie took the tattered photograph, holding it carefully by the edges. She stared at it for what seemed a long time, and her eyes glistened with tears.

"Our family," she murmured, her voice growing husky. "It's all of us." She stood and threw her arms around Violet, enveloping her in a fierce hug. "Our family," she repeated.

Violet held her tight. "It's going to be all right." Her voice sounded husky, too. "Now that we know for sure, we'll figure the rest of it out."

The precious photo trembled in Maddie's hand, and Landon rescued it. "Maybe when the two of you are finished being so mushy with each other, we can figure out if there are any clues in this photo."

Maddie released her, blinking the tears away. "That's Landon. Always businesslike."

"I see that," Violet agreed. But Landon hadn't been so businesslike in the attic just a few minutes ago.

"Do you have a magnifying glass, Violet?" He sounded calm and practical, but there was something in his eyes when he looked at her that brought the blood back to her cheeks.

"I think so. Let me look for it." She hurried out of the room, relieved to be away from his disturbing presence for at least a little while. There should be a magnifying glass in the desk in the den, but even after a prolonged rummage she couldn't locate it.

Lupita must have heard her, because she came out of

the kitchen, wiping her hands on a towel. "Violet? Are you looking for something?"

"I thought there was a magnifying glass in the desk, but I can't find it."

"It's here, in the kitchen drawer." Lupita produced it in an instant. "I use it to read the small print on labels. Why do you need it?"

"We've found something." She linked her arms with Lupita's. "Come and see."

Now that her first emotional response had passed, Violet felt excitement rising. Who knew what this discovery might lead to?

They went into the living room arm in arm. Maddie and Landon were standing together at one of the end tables, looking down at the photo, and a strand of Landon's blond hair had fallen onto his forehead. She should not be feeling an urge to press it back into place.

"Let me show it to Lupita," she said.

Landon and Maddie stepped back, and she led Lupita to the table. "Look."

"Ah." Lupita let out a long exhale. She looked from Violet to Maddie. "There you are—such beautiful babies." Her eyes filled with tears. "If only we could have known..." She stopped, shaking her head.

"I know," Violet said softly. "But at least Maddie and I are together now. Maybe soon we'll know why they separated us to begin with."

Violet took the glass and bent over the picture, eyeing it carefully. "Magnifying it doesn't really help much. The quality of the picture has deteriorated. It probably wasn't very good to begin with."

Maddie took the magnifier. "Let me see." She studied it for a long moment, but then she shook her head and handed it to Landon.

Violet tried not to smile. Landon had obviously been itching to get his hands on the magnifying glass and see for himself, not content to take their word for it.

Finally he straightened, shaking his head.

"Isn't there something we can do with it?" Maddie asked impatiently. "Can't we use some photo software to make it clearer?"

"That's not a job for an amateur with a fragile photo like this one," Landon said. "I know a little about it, but not enough. But I do know someone who could at least restore the photo and make copies for you, even if he can't bring out any more details. Will you let me take it back to Fort Worth with me and have him work on it?" He was looking at Violet for permission. "I promise I'll take good care of it."

Much as she hated to part with the photo, that solution made sense. "All right. Are you going back to Fort Worth right away?" She tried to sound as if it didn't matter to her when he left.

"Tomorrow," he said. "I do have to go back then so I can meet with a new client on Monday morning, but I'll be back as soon as I can. Maybe I could take you two out to dinner tonight, if you like."

Violet exchanged glances with Maddie, but she didn't seem to object. "That would be nice. But it will have to be on the early side. I need to be at Teen Scene again tonight."

She gave Landon a defiant glance, wondering if he had anything else to say on the folly of inexperienced volunteers working with teens.

But he just nodded. "Great. I'll make a reservation, then. Any suggestions?"

She smiled. "There aren't a lot of options in Grasslands, trust me. Sally's Barbecue is probably best.

She'll be pleasantly surprised to have someone actually call her for a reservation." Obviously, Landon was accustomed to far more fancy restaurants than anything Grasslands had to offer.

Landon nodded, glancing at his watch. "I'd best get out of your way so you can head up to Amarillo. I'll meet you at Sally's at around 5:30, if that gives us enough time before Teen Scene opens."

Us, he'd said. She decided not to read anything into that. "It's fine," she said. "We'll see you there."

Chapter Nine

Violet was smiling as she unlocked the side door at the church that evening. After the emotional strains of the day, supper with Landon and Maddie had been surprisingly relaxing. She and Maddie had come straight to the church after supper, but Landon had stopped by the hotel to change into something more casual.

"That was fun, wasn't it?" Maddie, entering the church in her wake, seemed to be on the same wavelength. "Landon was more relaxed than I've seen him in a long time."

"You sound as if you've gotten over being mad at him." Violet tried to keep her voice casual as she switched on the lights.

"I guess I can never stay mad at him for long," Maddie said. She gave Violet a second glance as they went down the stairs to the gym area. "Why?"

Violet shrugged. "He's a nice guy. I know you said your engagement was over, but…"

"I meant it," Maddie said firmly. "Why is that so hard to believe? Yes, he's a great guy, but he's not the one for me. The only time we even kissed was that night he proposed, and there wasn't a single spark. We were both dumb to even consider marriage. Landon was trying to help me, because that's who he is, and I was feeling sorry for myself and lost. But I'm not anymore." Suddenly she grabbed Violet's arm and pulled her around to face her. "You're interested in him, aren't you?"

It might have sounded accusing, but Maddie's face was lit up, her voice filled with mischief.

"No, no, I..."

Violet let that trail off, because Maddie was grinning at her knowledgeably.

"Come on, admit it. You're interested."

"You're not upset?" She clutched her sister's hand, looking into her eyes. "Please, Maddie, you have to be honest with me about it."

"Upset?" Maddie rolled her eyes. "Why would I be upset? I think it's great. I don't want Landon for a husband, but I wouldn't mind having him for a brother-in-law."

"Stop." Violet made a gesture of covering her ears. "It's nothing like that."

"Then what is it?" Maddie teased. "Come on, you can tell me. I'm your twin."

She shouldn't, but the urge to confide in someone was just too strong. "We...well, we kissed. That's all. It doesn't have to mean anything."

Maddie shook her head decisively. "I don't think Landon would kiss you unless it meant something. Not under the circumstances."

"That's just it. This isn't the right time for...well, romance. Not with everything that's happening."

"There is no right time," Maddie declared. "Promise me that you won't discourage Landon just because of what happened between him and me."

Someone was knocking at the outside door she hadn't unlocked yet, maybe Landon.

"All right," Violet said hastily when she saw the unrelenting look on her sister's face. "I promise. Now let go. I have to open up."

Maddie grinned triumphantly. "Don't forget. And tell me everything."

She wouldn't promise that, Violet decided as she hurried to the door. Not everything. She unlocked the door and swung it open, prepared to face Landon.

But it was Sadie Johnson, the new church secretary, standing there peering in anxiously.

"Sadie, hi. Come in, please."

Sadie sidled a few inches forward, clutching that drab sweater around her. She wore it like a protective coating, it seemed to Violet.

"I won't take up much of your time. He...Pastor Jeb, I mean...he asked me to come by and see that you have all the help you need tonight. He said to tell you he can come if you need him."

Maddie had moved next to her, and Violet felt sure Maddie hadn't missed the awed note in Sadie's voice when she said Jeb's name.

"Come on inside, Sadie." Maddie put her arm around Sadie and propelled her onto the balcony that overlooked the gym floor. "So tell us, do you like working for Pastor Jeb?"

Violet gave an inward sigh. Apparently there was no end to Maddie's matchmaking urges.

"He's...it's very nice," Sadie said, her eyes wide behind the oversized glasses.

She had lovely eyes, Violet realized, a deep, translucent green. What a shame that they were hidden behind those ugly glasses.

"Pastor Jeb is a sweetheart," Maddie declared.

Sadie blushed, but didn't answer. Violet decided she'd better intervene before teenagers started piling in on them. That would probably scare Sadie to death.

"I think we're okay for volunteers. Tell Pastor Jeb I'll call for help if I need it." In fact, Tim and Lynn Cole had just come down the stairs, and Violet waved to them. "Thanks for coming by, Sadie. I'd love to have coffee with you one day next week so we can get better acquainted."

She didn't have a spare minute in her schedule at the moment, but the spirit of welcoming newcomers had been thoroughly inculcated by Belle and Lupita between them.

"That…that's nice of you, but I don't think I can. I mean, my new job…" Sadie let that trail off, maybe realizing how silly it sounded.

"I'll call you," Violet said, and turned away to check in three teenage boys with a basketball who were eager to hit the court. When she looked back, Sadie was gone.

"She likes him," Maddie whispered in her ear.

Violet smiled, shaking her head. "Pastor Jeb has that effect on women," she said. "When he came the number of female volunteers for church activities soared, according to Mom."

"I'm not surprised," Maddie replied. "He's sweet. And Sadie could be attractive if she'd do something with herself."

"Don't matchmake," Violet warned. "That always backfires." She pointed to the small table and chair next to the door. "Here's your duty station. Get names when kids come in. They can leave anytime they want, but they have to check out with you. Mark down the time. Once they leave, they can't come back in."

The rule had been Pastor Jeb's idea, and it was a good one. It discouraged kids from telling their parents they were at Teen Scene and then heading for less worthwhile activities.

"Yes, boss." Maddie gave her a mock salute. "I'll man the gates until relieved. Landon should be here soon."

She sounded a little too innocent with that comment, Violet decided.

"Don't you dare say anything to him about what I told you," she warned.

"Wouldn't dream of it," Maddie replied, but her eyes twinkled. Deciding that saying anything else would just invite more teasing, Violet fled.

Landon glanced at his watch. Another hour and the teen center would be closing. He wasn't exactly longing for this evening to be over, but he had to confess to a sense of…what was it? Inadequacy? As much as he'd done to support missions to teenagers, donating generously and serving on the boards of two projects, he'd never had quite this up-close an experience.

It was one thing to donate money in Jessica's memory. It was quite another to see her face in the young girls who pressed together in close-knit circles, giggling, talking, eyeing the boys who pretended to be oblivious of them. Being here brought his grief to the surface—grief and guilt. If he had paid more attention to Jessica, she might be alive. He'd known from an early age that they couldn't count on their parents for that attention. He should have intervened.

He didn't belong here, Landon thought suddenly. He could play a pick-up game of basketball with the boys, of course, but what good did that do?

Maddie seemed to have adapted to this activity with

surprising ease, he realized. Right now she was at a corner table, talking to a slight young teenager over a couple of sodas. The girl had long, glossy black hair and a delicate face. It was the girl he'd seen crying.

Was this the girl Maddie had meant in her tirade against him this morning? The one about whom Violet was worried? If so, Maddie seemed to be making some progress with her.

He sensed someone beside him and turned to see Violet watching the pair, just as he was.

"Maddie seems to be fitting right in," he said.

"You sound surprised." Violet glanced up at him and then looked quickly away.

But not before he'd seen the warmth in her gaze. It gave him a totally irrational urge to put his arm around her.

He restrained himself. "Well, volunteering in a small-town teen center is a far cry from her glamorous job as assistant at *Texas Today* magazine."

"Maddie has unexpected depths," Violet said, smiling a little, but then the smile slipped away. "She talked to me about losing her job. That really devastated her."

"Do you recommend corralling a bunch of teenagers as a cure?" he asked.

Violet's head tilted as she seemed to consider the question. "I don't know about that, specifically. But I know it's important to feel that you're doing something useful, and she is."

"You make a good point." He let his hand brush hers between their bodies, trusting that no one else could see. The kids probably shouldn't see their chaperones holding hands. "Is that the girl Maddie said you were worried about?" he asked quietly.

She nodded. "Tracey Benton. The family is fairly new

in the area. They moved here from somewhere in south Texas."

"Trouble at home, do you think?" He glanced at the girl, who was smiling at something Maddie had said.

"I'm beginning to think so. Usually if they're upset about friends or boys, they'll come out with it, given half a chance. Something tells me this is family trouble."

"You really care, don't you?"

She glanced up, obviously surprised. "Of course."

"Even if the girl doesn't let you help her?"

Violet shrugged. "She still shows up every time we're open. As long as she's here, we have a chance to minister to her. There's no way of knowing how and why God might work through us."

Landon was silenced by the words. He made careful, thorough studies of any organization before he donated to it, as meticulous as if he were making a business investment. Violet's haphazard approach was foreign to his nature, but he still couldn't help but appreciate it.

"Well, Maddie seems to have things in hand here," Violet said. "I'm going to relieve Lynn on the door. It gets busy when a lot of kids start to leave at once."

She moved off, and Landon stood looking after her. Violet kept surprising him, showing him different aspects of herself that both startled and delighted him.

He checked out the kitchen to make sure the volunteer there didn't need any help, then walked back through to the gym, telling himself he wasn't necessarily doing that because Violet was there.

Violet was there, all right. She stood at the door, her body language eloquent. She was barring entrance to three teenage boys who loomed over her.

He walked quickly toward her, thinking of nothing but the need to protect her. As he came up to the group by the door, she was lecturing the kid who was obviously the ringleader of the trio. Taller than Violet by a half a foot, he teetered a bit on the heels of his Western boots, hat pushed back on his head.

"You know the rules, Sam Donner. Once you leave, you can't come back in."

"But I just went out to check on Danny, here." He shoved the kid next to him. "Danny forgot he was supposed to meet us here."

"You went out looking for beer," Violet said, her tone uncompromising. "And you smell like you found it. Now leave before I call your parents."

It hung in the balance for a moment. Violet's assumption of control seemed to be working. Then the taller of his two buddies prodded Sam in the ribs. "You gonna let her talk to you like that? You said we could have some fun here."

That gave the kid a bit of courage. He took a step toward Violet, opened his mouth, and closed it with a snap as Landon moved Violet aside with one hand and grabbed Sam's collar with the other.

"You've been asked to leave, fellas. I think you probably want to do just that, don't you?" He pulled up on the collar, the slightest movement making the kid stumble. Violet was right—he'd been drinking, and the smell of it churned Landon's stomach, sending memories tumbling through his mind. "Right?" He yanked the collar a bit harder, judging that none of them really wanted a fight, especially not with someone more than their size.

"Landon," Violet murmured, but Landon didn't take his eyes off the kid's face.

"Right, right, we're going." The kid tried to manage a smile, not quite succeeding. Landon let him go, and he stumbled backward out the door. "Come on. We'll find our fun somewhere else." He turned with an assumption of arrogance that didn't quite fly and shuffled off with his friends.

Landon closed the door on the heat and humidity, his stomach still churning. He turned to Violet to find her looking at him with fury in her eyes.

"What do you mean by interfering?" she snapped. "If I'd needed help, I'd have asked for it. Which I didn't."

Violet was still fuming inwardly as she finished the routine of closing Teen Scene down for another week. If she'd been able to say everything she was feeling at the time, she'd probably have simmered down by now.

But she hadn't, both because she wouldn't do that where there was a possibility of the teens overhearing, and because it just wasn't in her nature to blow up at anyone. How could Landon move her to both longing and fury so easily?

Maybe she didn't want to look too closely at the answer to that question.

Violet walked back through the gym, making sure everything had been cleaned up. She had it on good authority that a couple of church members had taken to checking out the rooms on Sunday mornings, ready to complain about the program if they found anything amiss. She was determined that they wouldn't.

The gym was fine, the kitchen cleaned up and everything put away. The games room and social room seemed to be in order as well. She began locking doors, making her way around methodically while wondering where Maddie had gone. She must have already headed upstairs.

Everything secure, she turned off the lights and

started up the stairs. Still no Maddie. Violet stepped outside and locked the door.

She turned, looking automatically for Maddie's car, but the space was filled instead by Landon's vehicle, with Landon standing beside it.

He straightened, probably reading the annoyance in her face even in the glow from the light above the door. "Don't be mad," he said quickly.

"Where's Maddie?"

"I asked if she'd let me bring you home so we can talk."

It wouldn't have been hard for him to persuade Maddie, given her obvious desire to bring the two of them together.

"It's late, Landon. I don't want to talk right now."

"But I do." He stepped toward her, and as he came into the circle of light, she was shocked by the pain in his face. "Please, Violet. Take a walk with me. I've got to get this out of my system before I bury it again."

The grief in his voice struck her heart so hard she felt it like a physical pain. Wordless, she held out her hand to him. He clasped it, holding on tight, and they turned and walked along the side of the church toward Main Street.

Landon stopped when they reached the street, as if unsure where to go. Then, still clasping her hand, he led the way across to the green, serene and quiet, its linden trees spreading their branches like arms in welcome.

The bench in the center of the green bore a plaque saying it was donated in memory of Uncle James, and that seemed comforting. Landon sat down next to her and Violet waited, half-afraid to hear what he had to say.

Crickets rasped their monotonous sound, and a light breeze tickled the hairs on her nape. A car went by, its radio playing a country-western song, and then they were alone.

"You think I shouldn't have interfered tonight with those boys. Maybe I shouldn't have, but..." He paused, seeming to search for words. "It's not something I talk about, but you deserve to hear what drives me. We've gotten too close, and everything that's happened since I came to Grasslands has been bringing up memories."

Painful memories, judging by the look on his face, and her heart was swept with the longing to wipe away that pain. If all she could do was listen, then she would. "Tell me," she said quietly.

His fingers tightened on hers. "I don't know if you can understand a family like mine. Two parents, plenty of money, two healthy children...from the outside we must have looked like the perfect family."

He fell silent, and she realized she'd have to prompt him to keep him going.

"Not so perfect on the inside?" she asked gently.

He shook his head. "Don't get me wrong. Our parents weren't abusive or anything of the kind. They just didn't have any time for us."

"Us?"

His hand moved restlessly, and for a moment she thought he'd jump up and run away from telling her. The desire was so strong in him that she could feel it.

"Jessica. My sister, three years younger than I." His voice softened. "She was such a beautiful little kid—blond curls, big blue eyes, such a sweet, innocent smile. Anyone would love her. Our parents just..." He shrugged. "Dad was totally involved with his business. Our mother was totally involved with her social life. We were left to a succession of housekeepers to take care of.

I figured out early on that if anyone was going to look after Jessica, I'd be that person."

Maddie had said his sister died when she was in her teens. A cold hand seemed to grip Violet's heart. "Something happened to her, didn't it?"

He was staring straight ahead, and his profile was sharp and forbidding...and as still as if it was carved from rock. He swallowed, and even in the semidark she could see the movement of his Adam's apple.

"She was just fourteen—the age of some of those kids tonight. Mom and Dad were off on a trip to New York, leaving the housekeeper in charge. Jessica had been driving me crazy all week, wanting to go with me to a football game and party." He scrubbed a hand across his face. "I told her I wouldn't because the kids would be too old for her, but the truth was that there was a girl I was interested in, and I didn't want my kid sister tagging along. So I went off without her."

He took a ragged breath. "As soon as the housekeeper dozed off, Jessica slipped out. She left me a note, saying she could find parties on her own and she'd tell me all about it the next day. But she didn't." He stopped, and she saw the muscles work in his neck. "She got into a car with a drunken kid. He ran right into a bridge abutment. He walked away with barely a scratch. She died a few hours later at the hospital, with nobody there but me."

She hurt so much for him that she could hardly breathe. So much pain, so much guilt—it flowed from him in heavy, suffocating waves, nearly burying her.

She couldn't speak, but she had to. She put her hand on his arm, the muscles so tight that they felt like steel cables. "Landon, it wasn't your fault. You—"

"I should have taken care of her. I didn't. She died." His voice was flat.

"You weren't her parent." She tried again. "Just her brother. Just a kid yourself. You couldn't have known what would happen."

"I should have taken her with me. She loved to go places with her big brother." He turned to her then, his face tortured. "But I didn't. I let her go off on her own and get in a car with a kid who was blind drunk."

"That's why you reacted so strongly to Sam and his friends." He'd seen her threatened by a drunken kid, and he'd jumped in to protect her in the way he hadn't protected his sister.

"I had to protect you. Just like I was trying to protect Maddie when I proposed to her. But nothing can make up for what I did to Jessica."

"Landon, I understand. I do. But you weren't responsible. Even if you had been, even if you'd been driving that car, you must know that Jessica would have forgiven you in an instant. That God forgives you." She smoothed her hand along his arm, hoping the simple human touch would comfort him.

He shook his head. "God may forgive me. But I don't forgive myself."

"Don't, Landon." Her voice shook and she tried her best to steady it. She couldn't pretend to have the strongest faith in the world, but this she was sure of. "You can't turn away from forgiveness that way. If you can't forgive yourself, how can you accept God's forgiveness?"

He looked at her bleakly. "I don't know. Maybe I can't."

She touched his face, smoothing her palm along his cheek, feeling warm skin and the faint stubble of beard. A muscle twitched in his jaw as if in protest to her touch.

Then he made an inarticulate sound and pulled her

into his arms, holding her fiercely, as if she was his only anchor from the pain that was sweeping him away.

She wrapped her arms around him, holding him close, thinking of how he had held her in those moments after she'd found the photo of her family. She didn't know what he felt for her. She only knew that at this moment he needed comfort, and if that was all she could ever give him, at least she would give him that right now.

Chapter Ten

Violet sat in church on Sunday morning, her gaze focused on Pastor Jeb. He stood tall in the simple, pale oak pulpit, his red hair like a flame where a shaft of sunlight from an upper window struck it. Around them, Grasslands' faithful crowded the plain, uncushioned pews of the simple sanctuary, its stained-glass windows the only ornamentation other than the painting of Jesus in Gethsemane above the communion table.

Having Maddie sitting next to her was a new experience, and her heart filled with thankfulness that she was reunited with her twin after all these years. It still seemed impossible that they should have found each other. Still, with God, all things were possible.

She wasn't quite so thankful for the attention they were arousing. People were too polite to turn around and stare openly in church, but those seated behind her and Maddie had a clear view. She could almost feel the numerous eyes on the back of her neck.

Violet brought her wandering thoughts back to the sermon, but Pastor Jeb's words about the power of prayer for even the smallest things in life sent them careening off on another tangent. Of course, Landon's grief over his lost sister wasn't small. It loomed large in his past, still coloring all that he thought and did.

He was taking all the responsibility for what happened to his sister on himself. That was a natural reaction to so painful a loss, but she'd think time and distance would have helped him see that other people bore responsibility, too.

His parents, for instance, to say nothing of the housekeeper who'd dozed off and let Jessica go out that fateful night. Then there were the people who'd given that party and obviously not provided enough supervision, and of course, the drunk driver himself.

And finally, Jessica. Much as it would pain Landon to think about it, a fourteen-year-old should be old enough to exercise caution about getting into a car with someone who was obviously drunk.

She couldn't have said any of those things to Landon last night. Maybe she never could. Landon had been silent as he drove her back to the ranch, as if the effort of telling her had exhausted all his words. She'd been as quiet, not knowing what to say that would do any good. It seemed that the odd way they had been brought together had led them into a closer relationship than would normally be possible in such a short period of time. She'd betrayed her deepest emotions to Landon, and last night he'd told her things he might never have told anyone.

Maybe it was too much, too fast. Maybe that was why he'd been so uncommunicative. Doubts swept through her. Maybe he'd been having regrets about saying anything at all to her.

When they'd reached the house, he'd walked her to the door, told her he'd be back in a few days at most, and given her a quick, hard kiss. Then he'd gotten into the car and driven away.

At least now she knew why he'd reacted the way he had to young Sam and his buddies. How could he do otherwise?

They stood for the closing prayer, and then Pastor Jeb raised his arms as if to encircle all of them in a hug. "God be with you until we meet again."

Somehow her heart eased as she repeated the words in her heart to her mom, to Jack, to Landon, even to the father she hadn't met.

The postlude rang out, and she and Maddie began to edge their way out of the pew. Their progress was impeded by all the people who wanted to satisfy their curiosity by having a word with them.

That was an uncharitable thought, and she scolded herself for it. These people were her neighbors and her church family. Of course they were interested, but they were well-meaning, too. Most of them honestly just wanted to welcome Maddie to their midst.

Glancing back toward the double doors, Violet noticed someone else who was in church for the first time that day. Tracey sat in the corner of the back pew, looking around as if unsure what to do next.

Violet murmured an apology in Maddie's ear and, ignoring her reproachful expression, deserted her, slipping back along the aisle. She nodded and smiled as people spoke to her and evaded the hands that reached out to her. She wanted to get to Tracey before the girl had a chance to disappear.

Violet reached the back of the sanctuary just as Tracey slipped out the door, taking advantage of a large woman who'd stopped to talk to Pastor Jeb to slide past without greeting him. Violet followed her, touching Tracey lightly on the shoulder.

The girl turned, her eyes wide and startled.

"Hey, Tracey, it's so nice to see you here today. I'm glad you decided to worship with us this morning."

Tracey nodded, her expression guarded. "I just thought I would. I mean, since I come here for Teen Scene, the church didn't seem so strange to me."

That was exactly the argument she'd used to sway some of the board members into starting the ministry, and she was glad to hear the reasoning coming from Tracey's lips. Tracey had obviously dressed carefully for her first appearance in church, discarding her usual jeans and T-shirt for a yellow cotton sundress. Her dark hair shone against the sunny color.

"I'm glad you feel at home here." She hesitated, wanting to ask but not wanting to offend. "Would your parents like to come, do you think?"

Tracey shook her head, looking down. "Mama prays a lot, but she said no when I asked her. And Daddy doesn't hold much with church people."

"Calls us a bunch of do-gooders?" Violet grinned. "That's okay. We're glad you're here, anyway." Other people were flowing out of the sanctuary now, and she edged Tracey over onto the grass, away from them, not wanting to be interrupted now that the girl was finally opening up to her.

"I wish they'd come," Tracey said in a sudden burst of confidence. "They'd like Pastor Jeb. Nobody could help liking him, don't you think?"

"I'd say so. I'm sure he'd be happy to go and visit them, if you think that might help."

Tracey shook her head decisively, her black hair flying out with the strength of the movement. "Please don't ask him that, Ms. Vi. It…they argue too much already. I don't want to make it worse." She clamped her lips together, as if wishing she could have those words back. "I didn't…I shouldn't have said that."

"It's okay." Violet touched her hand lightly. "I'm your friend, Tracey. You come first with me, not your parents. It's tough if they're fighting a lot, I know. Any time you want to talk, I'm here."

"I'm okay," Tracey said, trying to smile. "Lots of kids have parents who fight." She hesitated. "Ms. Vi, if my mama decided to go back to Mexico, would I have to go with her?"

For an instant it took her breath away. So that's what Tracey had been worrying about. She prayed silently for the right response.

"Do you think your mother plans to do that?"

Tracey shrugged, face downcast. "I don't know for sure. But I heard her say something about going back one time when she and Daddy were quarreling, and it made me scared. Would I?"

Unfortunately, Violet had no idea to the legalities of a situation like this. "I think that you and your daddy would have something to say about it, Tracey. It wouldn't be right for her to just take you away. Do you want me to find out what the law is about that?"

Tracey's eyes went wide with fear. "I don't want to get into trouble, or to get Mama into trouble."

"No, no, you wouldn't. I wouldn't mention your name. I can just find out what you should do if that happens. Okay?"

She didn't move for a moment, long enough for Violet to wonder if she'd said all the wrong things. Then Tracey threw her arms around Violet in a quick hug.

"Thank you," she whispered into Violet's ear. Then she turned and rushed off in a swirl of yellow.

* * *

"You're working overtime," Landon observed as he opened the door to his condo to find Dave leaning against the doorjamb. He stepped back, gesturing for the P.I. to come in.

"You told me to go all out," Dave reminded him. He stood for a moment in the living room, looking out the bank of windows that gave a view of downtown Fort Worth. From this height the city spread out like a magical place, especially at this hour, when dusk drew in and the lights came on.

"Quite a view." Dave relaxed onto the black leather couch. Everything in the room was either black or white, and Landon realized he was comparing it unfavorably with what he'd seen of the Colby ranch house. Here, everything was new, sleek and impersonal. There, the furnishings might be a bit worn, but there was welcoming warmth to the casual earth tones and bright accents.

He sat down opposite the PI. "I don't suppose you came here to admire the view. What's up?"

"After I got your message about the photograph, I quit chasing shadows. Like you said, it's obvious that the woman known as Belle Colby was Wallace's first wife and the mother of the two sets of twins."

"You got the photocopy I sent you?" At Dave's nod, he went on. "I turned it over to Phil O'Hara at Optical Graphics. If anyone can do anything with it, he can. But I'm not sure it gets us any further. It can't explain why they split up the twins, or why she's been living under an assumed name."

Dave reached out to toy with the chain of the pewter lamp on the glass-topped end table. "That's how I've been thinking, too. So I started at this end, trying to trace Belle Colby back as far as I can."

Landon nodded, a little discouraged. Even if Dave did produce some answers, what difference was it going to make at this point?

"Right. You told me before she seemed to have done an expert job of creating a new identity."

"It's beginning to look like more than that." Dave sat forward, his lean face expressing as much concern as he ever showed. "We've run into a blank wall, period. Belle Colby and her kids appear on the grid in Arkansas when the little girl was about a year old and the boy three. Oh, their identities are impeccable on paper, all right. Too impeccable."

"So what does that mean?" He had the sense that Dave was building up to something.

Dave spread his hands. "That means we know it's phony, but I doubt very much that we can ever get past it."

"So that's a dead end." He leaned back and realized he was thinking of Violet and Maddie, sitting on either side of their mother's hospital bed, waiting and praying for her to wake up.

"I'm not sure it makes a whole lot of difference, anyway," he said slowly. "Belle Colby may regain consciousness and tell the twins what they need to know. And Brian Wallace is bound to reappear from that mission trip of his at some point. He must know the answers as well."

"You want me to give it up, then?" Dave asked.

Landon knew from Dave's expression that he hated admitting defeat.

"Let's not write it off entirely," he said. "If anything else surfaces, you'll be in position to look into it."

"Okay, will do." Dave stood, and Landon walked with

him to the door. "Sorry I couldn't come up with all the answers."

Landon managed a smile, even though he didn't feel much like it. "I don't suppose we ever get all the answers. As long as we have enough to go on with."

He kept thinking of that after Dave left, and he walked restlessly over to the windows. It was darker now, and the lights shone more brightly. Out there, people were going home to families, going out for the evening, meeting friends. He could call someone or go out somewhere, but he couldn't kid himself. The only place he really wanted to be was a five-hour drive away.

He hadn't spoken to Violet since he'd dropped her off Saturday night. After he'd told her things he never talked about to anyone, not even Maddie.

He hadn't had a choice. He'd seen her face when he dealt with that drunken kid—she'd been angry that he'd interfered, but it was more than that. She'd looked at him as if she didn't know him, and he couldn't handle that feeling.

When he'd told her about Jessica, Violet had reacted with warmth and caring, but she hadn't been able to understand his guilt, not fully. He wasn't sure he did himself.

His email ding sounded, and Landon was relieved to return to his desk, shutting out the disturbing thoughts. He sifted through several unimportant items and saw a message from Phil O'Hara—a message with an attachment.

If nothing else, he might have a decent photo of her family to give Violet. He clicked on the attachment. The photo came up, startling him with its clarity. Phil really could work wonders.

Landon looked more closely, noticing details he hadn't

been able to see even with the magnifying glass. One detail in particular. There was a mailbox in the background, with the address stenciled on it. 21 Riley Street.

He leaned back in the desk chair, staring at the address. If the twins had been born in Fort Worth, that was probably a Fort Worth address. It wouldn't be that hard to find.

If he gave this to Maddie and Violet, he knew exactly what would happen. They'd take the bit between their teeth and charge into action, going to the address, asking questions, demanding answers.

He couldn't imagine what those answers might be, but everything in him revolted at the idea of sending those two rushing into that situation. He couldn't forget the implication of what Dave had found out. Belle Colby hadn't just split from her husband. She'd been involved in something so serious that she'd been forced to create a whole new identity for herself and two of her children. Something that might be heartbreaking to her children if they learned it from someone else—maybe even something that could be dangerous.

He couldn't do it. He clicked reply and typed a request, confident that Phil would be able to do what he wanted.

Violet and Maddie would have the photo of their family to cherish…but it wouldn't include that telltale address. He picked up the phone. In the meantime, Dave had something new to investigate.

Violet was on her way out the back door when the phone rang Wednesday afternoon. She turned back to answer it, unable to suppress a sliver of concern. Maddie had gone alone to see Belle, and if she'd found something wrong—

Violet picked up quickly. It wasn't Maddie. It was Pastor Jeb, and he sounded upset. He got right to the point.

"Someone broke into the Teen Scene area during the night. We didn't find the damage until just now. I've called the sheriff and he's on his way over. I thought you'd want to be here, too."

"I'll be right there." She was already reaching for her bag and her keys. "How bad is the damage?"

"Bad," he said soberly. "There's the sheriff now—I'll have to go."

Violet hung up. Her feet seemed glued to the spot. She didn't want to go. Didn't want to see what had been done.

But that was cowardly. She grabbed her bag and hurried out the hall, calling to Lupita that she'd be back later and not stopping for questions.

She raced out to the SUV, but before she could unlock it, she spotted the cloud of dust that meant another vehicle was coming down the lane. She looked, shielding her eyes.

The car pulled up next to her and Landon smiled at her. The smile faded as he saw her expression. "Violet? What's wrong?"

"Vandals. At the church." She began to feel that her tongue wasn't connected to her brain. "I'm sorry. I have to go."

"Get in. I'll drive you."

"You don't need—"

"You're upset. You shouldn't be behind the wheel. I'm coming anyway, and it makes more sense to let me drive you than to have me follow you."

Wordless, she went around the car and slid into the passenger seat. She'd resent his assumption of authority if not for the fact that he was probably right.

"I don't know why I feel so shaky at the news. It's not nearly as important as Mom's injury." She clasped her hands together.

"That's probably why." Landon went out the lane at a speed that had gravel spurting up, pinging against the underside of the car. "You've been running on nothing but nerve for too long. This is one thing too many."

She rubbed the back of her neck. He might have something at that. The least thing seemed to have the ability to drive her close to tears lately.

"Do you know how bad the vandalism was?" he asked.

"No. Just that it was in the area we use for Teen Scene. Do you think—surely none of the kids who come would do that!"

"No point in jumping to conclusions until you learn more." Landon reached into the back and grabbed something. Bringing it between the seats, he put a brown-paper-wrapped package in her lap. "A present for you."

She looked at him, but his gaze was on the road unfolding ahead of them. His clean, spare profile was unexpectedly dear to her.

She shifted her gaze to the package, afraid of giving herself away, and loosened the tape on it. She smoothed the paper back.

It was the photo of her family, restored to a condition that was probably better than it had been originally. The faces were clear—Belle smiling at the camera, Brian looking down at the little boy whose hand he held. Jack? But it could as easily be Grayson.

"Oh, Landon." Her voice choked. "It's wonderful. Thank you so much."

"It's nothing," he said, and there seemed to be a faint

reservation in his voice. "There are copies in the back for Maddie, Grayson and Jack as well."

"That was so thoughtful of you." She longed to clasp his hand in thanks, but that probably wasn't a good idea when he was driving.

He shrugged. "Forget it. I knew the right person for the job, that's all."

They were in town already, heading for the church, and her nerves tightened at the thought of what waited there. She tried to shake off the worry, looking at Landon instead.

"You haven't told me what you're doing back in Grasslands. You didn't need to drive all this way in order to deliver the photographs."

"I'm more trustworthy than the mail," he said lightly. "Besides, as I told you, I can run my business from anywhere, as long as I have an internet connection."

"And you find Grasslands an inspiring place in which to work?" she asked, trying to match his light tone.

He pulled into a parking space by the side door of the church and turned to give her a look that brought a flush to her cheeks. "I find it very inspiring," he said, in a voice that had suddenly grown husky.

Violet slid out quickly. "We...we'd better go inside." And she better figure out a way to control both her face and her voice before she saw anyone else.

Sadie met them in the hallway, looking more mouse-like than ever, eyes scared behind her glasses. "Pastor Jeb said to meet him downstairs," she said, glancing from Violet to Landon.

"Thanks, Sadie. We'll go right down." Somehow she always felt she had to be reassuring when she spoke with Sadie, but the effort made her feel a bit more under control.

Violet hurried down the stairs, aware of Landon close behind her. The Teen Scene's troubles really weren't his concern, but it was comforting to have someone on her side.

A chill struck her. Landon had expressed disapproval of the project the first time he'd come. Maybe he wasn't so completely on her side in this.

She was in the social room before she could analyze his reaction any further. She stopped, shocked. Vandalism, Pastor Jeb had said. She'd expected a few broken windows, maybe some pieces of furniture thrown around. This was more like wholesale destruction.

One couch had been slashed, its stuffing hanging out forlornly. The other had been splashed with red paint. The artist hadn't stopped there with the paint—it was splattered liberally over the rug and splashed on the walls, then used to write a few ugly words. The television had been smashed, leaving shards of glass on the floor.

Looking through the open doorway to the game room, she could see that the Ping-Pong table was broken—the legs wrenched off so that it tilted listlessly against the wall. A step forward showed her more of the room—the board games tossed from their shelves and scattered on the floor, the air-hockey table smashed almost beyond recognition.

Landon's hands came down on her shoulders, steadying her. "It sounds as if the pastor is in the gym," he said. "Maybe we should go in there."

She nodded numbly and let him propel her past the damage and into the gym. Pastor Jeb was there, talking with Sheriff George Cole, but he looked up to give her a reassuring smile. Coming to her senses and realizing they hadn't met, she introduced Landon to the two men.

"Landon is a friend of my sister's from Fort Worth,"

she added. "He helped us out at Teen Scene this past weekend."

Sheriff Cole eyed him for a moment, but then he nodded. "Glad you have somebody with you, Violet. This is an ugly thing to see, especially after you put so much work into the place and all."

She nodded, not wanting to think about all the hours of scrounging up cast-off furniture and begging for donations to cover the cost of paint and equipment. "Who could have done this? How did they even get in? We locked up when we left Saturday night, I know we did."

"Broke in that door with a crowbar, looks like," the sheriff said. "The pastor was telling me that's the door you use to let kids in here, that right?"

She nodded, not sure what he was driving at.

"Seems like it might have been done by someone who'd been here for that program of yours. They'd naturally come to that door. Anyone intent on doing damage to the church would head for the sanctuary, I'd think."

That made sense, much as she hated to admit it, and she looked at Sheriff Cole with renewed respect. He'd been on the force here for as long as she could remember, a sturdy, solid symbol of the law.

"I'd hate to think the kids we host would do something like that. Why would they want to destroy the place they come to for fun?"

Sheriff Cole shrugged. "Teens can take offense easily sometimes. Get the idea you weren't treating them right, or weren't doing enough. Or they were being just plain mean. Anyone you've had a run-in with?"

Her brain didn't seem to be working. It was Landon who spoke.

"There were three guys we had to kick out on Saturday night. They'd been drinking, and Ms. Colby wouldn't let them come back in. They didn't take it well."

"I don't think they'd do this," she protested, but of course she couldn't imagine anyone she knew doing such damage.

"You know the names?" The sheriff had his pen poised over his notebook.

She hesitated, not wanting to be the one to set the police on the kids.

"The ringleader was Sam something," Landon said, clearly not feeling any such reluctance. "I don't think I heard the others' names."

"Never mind, I can fill in the blanks. Sam Donner, along with his buddies Danny and Kevin, was it?" His keen eyes fixed on Violet's face, requiring an answer.

"Yes, that's right," she said. "But I still feel—"

The person who'd just entered gained their attention by the simple expedient of pounding his cane on the wooden floorboards. They all swung toward the sound.

Davis Stuart swept them with an ice-blue gaze, his eyes bright in his leathery face, his hair snowy under the Stetson he always wore. Violet could almost hear Pastor Jeb sigh. With Davis as the chair of his church board, the pastor didn't have many easy meetings.

"This has turned out exactly as I said it would," Davis said, "and you have no one to blame but yourselves for the results. Let riffraff into the Lord's house, and this is what you get. Maybe now you'll realize that it's time for this ridiculous project to end."

Chapter Eleven

Landon eyed the newcomer cautiously. Whoever he might be, he seemed to think he was important, in his own eyes, at least. The man had white hair and was immaculately dressed. He wielded that silver-headed cane like a weapon instead of an aid to walking.

"Davis." Pastor Jeb sounded resigned. "What brings you here?"

"I heard about the vandalism to my church, of course." His use of the pronoun seemed to indicate that the church belonged to him.

Violet had stiffened, as if preparing for an attack. Annoyance surged through Landon. Violet was already struggling enough. She didn't need more pressure. He took a step closer, wanting to help but not knowing how.

The movement seemed to draw the attention of the older man. He shifted his glare from the pastor to Landon. "Who's this?" he demanded.

"Landon Derringer, Davis Stuart," Pastor Jeb said briefly. "Landon has been helping us out with Teen Scene."

Stuart sniffed, seeming to think the introduction unworthy of comment. Landon walked to the man and held out his hand, determined not to let Stuart's rudeness affect his actions.

"Mr. Stuart. It's a pleasure to meet you." Actually, it didn't seem to be much of a pleasure, but courtesy helped oil the wheels of most human action, he'd found.

Looking thrown off his stride, Stuart shook hands briefly. Then he clasped his hands on the knob of his cane.

"Well, Pastor?" His tone sharpened. "How do you expect to pay for this mess? Or is Ms. Colby going to do it, since the whole misguided project was her idea?"

Landon could almost feel Violet wince. The Colby family seemed to do well enough, but he suspected that, like most ranchers, their finances were tied up in land and stock and equipment.

"It's a church project," he pointed out. "Surely the insurance will cover any loss."

Pastor Jeb looked stricken. "I wish that were so. But the insurance is really meant to cover us in the face of major destruction, like a fire. The deductible is so high that we can't count on it for something of this sort."

Of course. Like a lot of cash-strapped organizations, they'd taken every cost-cutting measure they could find, most likely.

"I don't know what your interest is, young man." Stuart's bristling white eyebrows lowered. "But the insurance won't cover the damage, and believe me, I intend to make sure that the church council doesn't sink any more of our funds into this misbegotten project. Throwing good money after bad, that's what it would be."

Landon was momentarily distracted by the old cliché, since Stuart said it with such determination.

"But we have to make repairs," Violet protested. "The kids will expect us to be open on Friday night."

Stuart reddened angrily. "Kids! Hooligans, more likely. They've done this, you can be sure of that."

"Now, Davis." The sheriff looked like a man who had dealt with Davis Stuart before. "You can't jump to conclusions like that without proof. This is a police matter. We'll find the guilty parties. That's our job."

"You won't need to look any farther than those young hoodlums who were here on Saturday night," he said, undeterred by the sheriff's wisdom. "There will be no more money spent on them by this church, I tell you. If Ms. Colby's so eager to entertain them, let her find another place."

"Teen Scene is a ministry of Grasslands Community Church." Pastor Jeb surprised Landon by the firmness in his tone. Apparently he was willing to go up against the local power broker for what he believed in. "We have no intention of deserting the program. Even if the guilty parties were in the building because of the teen program, and we don't know that, it wouldn't justify denying the program to all the other kids."

"Fine." Stuart's voice grated, and he thudded the cane on the floor for emphasis. "Just remember that I control the majority of the board. See how far you get without funds."

Violet was looking at Pastor Jeb, her eyes filled with gratitude, and the expression tugged at Landon's emotions. Maybe this program would be better run by a team of professionals, but it was pretty obvious Grasslands couldn't afford that. And Violet had sunk her heart into it. It wasn't fair to desert her when things went wrong.

Landon cleared his throat. "As it happens, I'm associated with a charitable foundation in Fort Worth," he said. "We provide grants for worthy projects that minister to teens. I feel sure we'd be willing to fund the necessary repairs to get the Teen Scene up and running again."

Davis Stuart was looking at him with ill-concealed hostility. Clearly he was used to running things in this church, if not the whole town.

"What's the name of this foundation?" he snapped. "Its board might not be so eager to help if I had a word with them."

"The Jessica Derringer Foundation," Landon said evenly. "Coincidentally, I *am* the board. I can assure you, the money will be here. Repairs can start immediately."

Stuart glared at him for another moment. Then, apparently conceding defeat, he turned and stomped toward the door, where he paused for one final remark. "I hope you know what you're getting yourself into, young man," he growled. He went out and let the metal door bang behind him.

"Well." Pastor Jeb said the word on a long exhale. "Davis was certainly in top form today." He turned to Landon, holding out his hand. "I'm not sure that we've done anything to merit your support, Landon, but we're mighty glad to have it. I can't thank you enough for your generous offer."

"Forget it," he said quickly. He turned to Sheriff Cole. "Sheriff, how long until your investigation is finished and we can start work in here?"

The sheriff considered, patting his paunch absently. "Well, I reckon we can get done in here this afternoon. You can start first thing tomorrow, if you can get a crew in here that quick."

"We will," he said confidently. "Thank you."

Pastor Jeb put his hand on Sheriff Cole's shoulder. "Let's have a look at the rest of the damage, shall we?"

He steered him toward the games room. "Violet, are you coming?"

"In a minute," she said, looking up at Landon with a question in her eyes. As soon as the other two were out of earshot, she asked it.

"Why?" she said simply. "I thought you didn't approve of our program. That you felt it should be run by professionals, not well-meaning amateurs."

"I realized something after I shot my mouth off that way," he explained. "I realized that I trust your judgment. And I'm willing to put my money where my mouth is."

Her eyes sparkled with unshed tears. "Thank you, Landon. Thank you."

Over supper, Violet had been telling Maddie about the vandalism, capping it with the story of Landon's charitable act.

"I couldn't believe he would offer to pay for the repairs, after what he'd said about our amateur efforts." Violet led the way into the den, where she and Maddie had formed the habit of sitting after supper. "It was so unexpected."

"Landon can be unexpected," Maddie said. She curled up in the corner of the sofa and pulled her laptop from the table onto her lap. "I suspect you had something to do with his change of heart."

"He did say he trusted my judgment." She gave Maddie a searching look. "You're sure that you don't mind—"

Maddie shook her head, smiling a little. "How many times do I have to say it? Landon was always like a big brother to me, and that's all he'll ever be." She leaned across to tap her knee. "Trust me on this. Landon never looked at me the way he looks at you."

Maddie turned to her computer, and they were silent for a few minutes as she checked her email. Violet leaned back in her corner of the sofa, thinking about Landon.

There had been little chance to talk to him alone after his offer. Once the sheriff had gone, they'd been closeted with Pastor Jeb and a few other members of the teen center board, assessing the damage, deciding what repairs were needed, talking to carpenters and plumbers, making plans.

She'd been impressed, seeing Landon in action that way. He'd taken full part in the planning, making it clear that he didn't want them to stint on the repairs but to get them done both quickly and thoroughly. He'd even managed to get Grasslands' only plumber to promise to make the bathroom repairs a priority. She wasn't sure how he'd managed to do that, and she spared a moment of regret for whoever had expected the plumber tomorrow.

"Finally," Maddie said suddenly. "I got an email from Carter."

Carter, the younger brother. Well, half brother, it seemed now.

"Is he all right?" Carter seemed a rather shadowy figure to her.

"Fine, apparently." Maddie was scanning the message. "He never talks about what he's doing. Well, I suppose he can't. The military doesn't want their officers to be giving away anything on what might be an unsecured wireless connection."

"What does he say? Did you tell him about...well, about us?"

Maddie shook her head. "It seems way too complicated to explain in an email. He'd have a million questions, and just be frustrated because he couldn't ask them."

"I suppose you're right," Violet said reluctantly. Somehow this would be a bit more real if Maddie's dad and brothers knew about it.

"So I told him I had some big news to share, but it would wait until he could call me. I asked if he'd heard anything from Dad. He says not for over a month, so that's no help."

"You've emailed our dad again?"

"Again and again," Maddie said. "And I've left messages on his cell phone. He has to be someplace where he doesn't have access, that's all I can figure."

"Isn't there some central organization that's in charge of this mission trip of his?" It seemed so odd that he'd be completely out of touch.

But Maddie shook her head. "He used to work directly with an organized group, but as he got to know more people in some of the impoverished areas, he went off on his own."

"So...he hasn't been around much for you?" Violet asked the question cautiously, wanting to know but not wanting to sound critical.

Maddie closed the computer with a snap. "I guess it does sound funny. I mean, in comparison to how close you've always been to your mother."

"Yes, I suppose it does." Violet seemed to see Belle sitting where Maddie was, leaning forward, her face alight with love, eager to hear about her day. Here, not in the hospital bed in Amarillo.

Maddie's forehead wrinkled. "You know, I guess when you're a kid, you just accept the way things are. We always knew that Dad's work was very important and that he had to be away."

"You never questioned that?" It didn't sound as if she'd missed a lot by not having Brian Wallace in her life.

Maddie considered. "Sometimes you hash over your relationship with your parents with your friends, especially when you're in college. I always had the feeling that Dad was sort of protecting himself from getting too close." She looked at Violet, her face serious. "I guess now I know why. Whatever happened between Mom and Dad, it had to be big, and I think it has affected Dad's relationship with us ever since."

"I wish I'd known him," Violet said softly.

"You will." Maddie grabbed her hand. "Just like I'll know Mom. He'll come back, and she'll wake up. You'll see."

Violet nodded. She had to believe that, but there was a lump in her throat.

"I know what," Maddie said. "Let's write letters to them, telling how it felt to find each other. You can write to Dad, and I'll write to Mom. Then, even if it's a while before they can read them, they'll know how we felt."

"That's a good idea." Violet smiled, but she suspected Maddie would do the same thing she would. She'd leave out the part about feeling angry and betrayed over all they'd lost.

One day, they'd be able to sort this out with their parents, but she didn't think it was going to be easy.

Violet and Maddie reached the church early the next morning. Violet had already consulted with both Ty and Ricardo, reassured by their ability and willingness to handle what needed to be done on the ranch.

But there had been an undercurrent to their conversations that she hadn't been able to dismiss. People who depended upon the Colby Ranch for their livelihood were too aware of the uncertainty of life in the Colby family right now.

Jack should return. She knew that…everyone knew that except, apparently, Jack. Ricardo had looked at her with sorrow in his eyes, even though he hadn't spoken of her brother. He was wondering why she hadn't called Jack to insist that he come home.

She'd have to. She knew that, but still she delayed, praying that he'd come back on his own.

The area outside the door into the church gym was crowded with vehicles—two pickup trucks, the plumber's paneled truck, a delivery truck from the lumberyard and another from the hardware store. Landon stood at the door in consultation with Pastor Jeb.

"Wow," Maddie murmured. "Looks as if someone's been working overtime."

"I wonder what Landon did to get all these people here already this morning." Violet felt faintly uneasy, as if she'd unleashed something she couldn't control.

"Don't ask," Maddie said, getting out of the car. "Just appreciate."

That was probably good advice. Now to follow it.

When they approached the door, Landon glanced at them, his face relaxing in a smile. "Have you come to supervise?"

"We've come to work," Maddie declared. "We're not going to sit back and let you have all the fun."

"The carpenters and plumbers are just getting started." There was a note of protest in his voice. "Maybe if you waited until later—"

"We're going to see Mom later. We'll start in the kitchen," Violet said firmly. "The only damage there was the graffiti. We'll get busy painting." She'd taken the precaution of bringing paint, brushes and rollers, and she didn't intend to be left out. This was her project, after all.

She was ready for a battle, knowing Landon's protectiveness, but she didn't get one. Maybe he knew better.

"Okay, sounds good," he said. "Need any help carrying stuff in?"

"We'll take care of it," Maddie said. "You get back to supervising, or whatever it is you're doing."

Chuckling, Landon turned away to answer a question from the plumber, and they went inside to check out the kitchen and bring their equipment in.

The spray paint on the walls and cabinets might have sent Violet's emotions spiraling downward again, but Maddie seemed determined not to let that happen. She kept up a steady stream of chatter while they scrubbed and wielded the brushes and rollers, forcing Violet to respond and keeping her from focusing on the destruction.

After only an hour, they had begun to see progress. The old kitchen, unused except for the teen center program, hadn't been repainted in years, and it seemed to come to life under the impact of fresh, new color.

"You know, this paint is making a huge difference." Maddie stood back, hands on her hips, surveying their progress. "I like the earth tones in here."

Violet looked at her and couldn't help grinning. "They're pretty becoming on you, too." Maddie had paint everywhere, including a streak down one cheek.

"Better watch out, or I'll decorate you as well," Maddie warned, flicking the brush at her.

"You two girls getting paint on the walls or just each other?" Harriet said from the kitchen doorway.

Violet stared. It wasn't just Harriet from the farm stand. Beyond her was a group of teenagers, peering around her to get a look at the kitchen.

"Sure is a mess." Joey Thomas hopped up onto the kitchen pass-through to get a better view.

"Get off there," Harriet chided. "You're going to make sure it's not a mess much longer. Maria and Janey, you set up a table in the gym with the lemonade and food we brought. Some of you boys find a table they can use. The rest of you, get in here and get busy. Painting, not messing around," she warned.

The kids scattered promptly in obedience, leaving Violet with no response but to stare at Harriet.

"But…the store?" she questioned.

"Don't you worry about a thing," the older woman said, tying a bright bandanna over her wiry hair. "I left Julie in charge. She might only be eighteen, but she knows what she's doing. I'll pop back later to check on her, but everything's fine. Now let's get busy."

Blinking unexpected tears out of her eyes, Violet murmured a silent prayer of thanks and turned back to the painting.

By the time she and Maddie had to start cleaning up to go to the hospital, with all those hands working, the kitchen was nearly done. Violet walked back through the gym, marveling at the people who were hard at work. Plenty of kids from Teen Scene, people from church, others she didn't even know—all of them had pitched in to help.

Her throat tightened. Some of these people lived hand-to-mouth, she knew. They might not be able to help with money, but they were giving their labor and support, and that meant more.

She walked on into the social rooms in search of Landon, weaving her way through people intent on their work. She found him in one of the restrooms, in consultation with the plumber. He glanced up.

"Violet, glad you're here. We're planning to run a vanity all across this wall. Joe here says he can do either a white laminate cabinet or natural wood. Which would you rather have?"

The two men stood looking at her, waiting, and her throat seemed too tight to speak.

"But...you don't have to do that. We can just keep that single basin. It wasn't damaged."

"As long as we're in here, we may as well do it right," Landon said.

"That's true enough, Violet." Joe Tyler, quite naturally, was eager to do the whole job. "You'll be a load happier with it in the long run."

Her gaze was fixed on Landon's face. "I know you... your foundation...is willing to pay for repairs, but I... we shouldn't take advantage of your generosity..." She stumbled over the words.

Landon stepped over Joe's tools, took her arm, and piloted her out of the restroom and into the adjoining hallway, empty at the moment.

"Listen," he said, holding both her arms in a warm clasp. "This is what the foundation was set up to do." Pain moved in his eyes for an instant. "Whenever we pick up a project, I think about what Jessica would have liked. Then I do it."

"But the expense..." She gazed up at him, still troubled.

He shook his head, his brow furrowed. "It's just money, Violet. Those people donating their time and labor are doing far more, believe me."

A little reassured, she smiled at him. "Only people who have plenty say things like, 'It's just money.'"

"True." He smiled back, his face easing. "The Bible says that the love of money is the root of all evil. I've given that a lot of thought since I became a Christian. I see people like my parents, who let money lead them into an unending pursuit of pleasure, only to be dissatisfied in spite of their possessions."

She nodded. "I guess I can understand that, but most people around here are just trying to get by."

"I decided a long time ago that money is a tool and it can be used wisely or foolishly. The foundation lets me use what's been entrusted to me wisely, I hope." His green eyes suddenly twinkled. "Now, please, let Joe get on with his work. Laminate or wood?"

How could she argue, given the depth of his feeling? "Natural wood, please," she said, returning his smile.

Chapter Twelve

The hospital was beginning to look too familiar, and Violet found she resented that as they walked down the hallway toward Belle's room. No matter how kind the staff was, and they were very kind, her mom should be at home, where she belonged.

"Violet?" Maddie touched her arm as they started into the room. "Are you all right?"

She nodded, trying to smile. "It's just hard to keep up a cheerful front all the time. You know?"

"I know." Maddie clasped her hand. "Every time I come in, I think this will be the day. This will be the day when she opens her eyes and looks at me, and she knows right away who I am."

Violet squeezed her hand, and they went into the room together.

There was no change. She saw that immediately. Belle lay exactly centered in the bed, the sheet drawn up and folded back at the top. Someone had taken the time to put her shoulder-length hair into two loose braids, and they formed dark auburn ropes against the white pillow.

"Mom, hi. Maddie and I are here to visit." Her attention was caught by a vase of red roses on the table next to the bed. "Wow, Mom. You must have an admirer. These roses are gorgeous. Did Jack send them?"

There was no answer, of course. She plucked the card out from the roses and opened it.

You are in my prayers. Landon Derringer.

She glanced across the bed at Maddie. "They're from Landon."

"I told you he could be surprising." Maddie clasped Belle's hand. "Would you like to smell the roses, Mom?"

"That's a good idea." Hadn't she read something about people still being able to smell, even when their other senses weren't working properly? Violet pulled one of the long-stemmed roses from the vase, careful of the thorns. She held it under her mother's nose. "There. Doesn't that smell lovely?"

"The color is gorgeous, too. It's such a deep, vibrant red. Landon sent them. He's a friend of mine from Fort Worth. Violet probably won't tell you this, so I will. She's crazy about him."

"I wouldn't go that far," Violet said, putting the rose back in the vase. "But he is...well, really special."

She turned away to pull the usual chair up by the bed, and Maddie did the same on her side of the bed.

"So," Maddie queried once she was seated, "how many guys have you called *really special* besides Landon?"

Violet wrinkled her nose. "Okay, none. But that doesn't mean anything will come of this relationship."

"Of course not." Maddie looked a tad smug. "We'll just wait and see. But if Mom were awake, what would she be saying right now?"

"I know exactly." Violet smiled at her mother's unresponsive face. "She'd say, 'Violet, just be sure when you give your heart to someone.'"

Maddie smiled as well, but then the smile faded. "I wonder if she felt really sure of Dad."

"She must have, don't you think?" Violet stroked her mother's hand. "But sometimes things happen that people can't control."

Maddie nodded, gazing at her mother's face. "How old is she, anyway? I never thought to ask that."

"Forty-three her last birthday."

"Really? That means she was only sixteen or seventeen when Grayson and Jack were born. Did she ever talk about that?"

"Just once, when I did some arithmetic and came up with that figure. I tried to use it as a lever when she didn't want me to go to some party with the older kids." Violet sighed ruefully, remembering that conversation. "Mom looked at me and said she didn't want me following in her footsteps in that regard. And she didn't let me go to the party."

"I wonder how much their youth had to do with their marriage breaking up." Maddie touched her mom's hand where a ring might have been at one time. "They were awfully young to be the parents of twins."

"That must have been hard. It wouldn't be surprising if they weren't mature enough to make a go of marriage."

Wake up, Mom. Answer the questions for us. Please.

The door swung open, letting in a doctor whose swift pace didn't alter until he glanced up and saw them sitting there. It was a man Violet hadn't seen before, in his fifties probably, with a pencil-thin moustache and an air of authority.

"Are you Mrs. Colby's children?" He glanced from one to the other. "Yes, I see that you are. You both resemble your mother very much, don't you?" His smile warmed a face that Violet had initially thought rather frosty.

"I'm Violet Colby," she said. "This is my sister, Maddie Wallace."

"Nathan Fremont," he said. "I've been thinking I should have a word with Mrs. Colby's family. Are there any other family members?"

"My brother, Jack." It was far too complicated, Violet decided, to bring up Brian Wallace and his sons.

"Your father is not in the picture?" he asked.

Violet shook her head. "Not now. You can talk to us about anything concerning our mother's care."

She could read the reluctance on his face, and a chill hand seemed to grip her heart. "Is something more wrong with Mom?" She had to choke the words out.

"No, nothing like that," Dr. Fremont said. "It's just usually the spouse who deals with the decisions that have to be made in this sort of case."

"What decisions?" Maddie sounded as scared as Violet felt.

He looked from Maddie to her. "Your mother is stable now, I'm sure you realize that. However, there's been no further progress in some time."

"That doesn't mean there won't be," Maddie said quickly.

He nodded. "True. But there comes a point when we have to accept the fact that there may not be any—that your mother may be in a persistent coma from which she won't recover."

Violet pressed her lips together, shaking her head. "I can't believe that. I won't."

"I understand." His voice was gentle. "You should always hang on to hope. The point is, however, that she no longer needs the type of specialized care we provide here. You need to start looking for another place—probably a nursing care facility, if there is one close to your home."

Violet could only stare down at her hands clasped in her lap. Maybe she should have expected this, but she hadn't. Everything in her objected. Surely there was something else the hospital could do. But the doctor had made it clear that there wasn't, and Violet felt herself sinking under the weight of the responsibility.

"How long do we have to make that decision?" Maddie seemed to sense that she'd have to take charge now. "We need time to find the right place for our mother, and we'll need to talk to our brother before we can make any arrangements."

"Of course." He sounded relieved. "We're not rushing you, but it is something that must be done. You should look into different facilities, ask around, talk to people who have used those facilities. We can discuss it again in a few days."

A few days—Violet's mind rebelled. She couldn't possibly be ready to make a decision that soon, not when it felt like giving up hope that her mom would get better.

The doctor seemed to take their silence as agreement. He nodded and walked away, maybe eager to leave now that he'd delivered his unpalatable news.

Maddie walked around the bed and touched Violet's shoulder. "It's not giving up," she said with that quick understanding that seemed to exist between them. "We'll find a good place that can provide all the therapy and support Mom needs. Maybe it will even be better."

Violet appreciated what Maddie was trying to do, but there was one immediate thought in her mind. She couldn't give Jack any more time to come to his senses.

"I have to call Jack." She got out her cell phone, and then realized she couldn't use it here.

"Why don't you go down to the lobby to call? Or even outside? I'll stay here with Mom."

"Yes, that's what I'd better do." Violet stood. "Thanks, Maddie. For…for sharing the burden."

"Hey, that's what twins are for, right?" Maddie gave her a little shove toward the door. "Go on, make the call. It's time Jack came home."

Everyone was agreed on that, Violet reflected as she rode down on the elevator. Everyone except, possibly, Jack himself. Well, he was out of options.

Not wanting to make the call where anyone might overhear, she went out through the sliding door, feeling the heat weigh her down as she reached the sidewalk. Walking a little distance from the main entrance, she found a bench in the shade and called.

She half expected the phone to go directly to messages, but instead Jack answered immediately.

"Vi? What's wrong? Is it Mom?" Fear filled his voice.

"There's been no change," she said quickly.

"Thank God," he murmured.

"But something else has come up. You have to come back."

"If this is about Maddie and her father—" he began.

"No." She cut him off. "It's about Mom. The doctor says that they can't do anything else for her at the trauma center." It was a struggle to keep her voice even. "We have to make arrangements to move her to a nursing home."

Silence for a moment, and she knew he was fighting against accepting that, just as she was.

"I don't know anything about nursing homes. Can't you and Maddie handle it?"

"Stop being selfish," she snapped, her temper frayed to the breaking point. "You went off and left me to deal with everything. This is one thing too much." Her voice shook suddenly. "I need you to come home, Jack. I need my big brother."

Silence for a moment.

"Hang on, Violet," he said, his voice gentle. "I'll be home tomorrow."

Landon was back at Sally's Barbecue again, and he had to confess he was getting a little tired of the menu. If he spent much more time in Grasslands, he'd have to make some other arrangements.

Was he going to spend much more time in Grasslands? A few weeks ago he'd have laughed at the idea. But then, a few weeks ago he hadn't known Violet.

At any rate, he expected a bit more from supper tonight. Not that Sally would have changed her menu, but he'd caught Violet on her cell phone when she was returning from Amarillo and convinced her to have dinner with him.

She'd sounded distracted, and he frowned as he parked his car. He'd had to resort to saying they needed to talk about the progress at Teen Scene before she'd agreed.

He couldn't help but smile as he thought about that phone call. He'd been able to hear Maddie's voice in the background, urging her to go to dinner with him. Maddie had to be the most generous former fiancée in history.

Landon had just gotten out of the car when Violet's SUV pulled in. She got out, wearing a turquoise sundress that made her creamy skin glow in comparison. Her hair wasn't in its usual ponytail—it hung to her shoulders like auburn silk. She took his breath away.

"Violet." He went to her quickly. "You look lovely."

She lifted her eyebrows. "Because I look more like Maddie?"

"No," he said truthfully. "Because you look like yourself."

The color came up in her cheeks. "I don't know what to say to that."

He took her hand and they walked toward the restaurant. "You don't have to say a thing, except that you enjoy being with me as much as I enjoy being with you. If it's true, of course."

"It is," she said softly.

By the time they were seated, Violet seemed to have recovered from her embarrassment. They ordered, and then he took a second look at her face. Happiness lurked in her eyes, surprising him.

"You look as if you've had good news. Is your mother better?"

"No, not that. I wish..." She let that trail off. "I'm just pleased because Jack is coming home."

Jack, the missing brother. "So he called you?"

"No. I called him."

The waitress arrived with platters of barbecue, and they were silent while she set them on the table and refilled their water glasses, exchanging some lighthearted banter with Violet and glancing at him with curiosity.

When she'd gone, Violet picked up her fork and then put it back down again. "You didn't ask why I called Jack," she said.

"I had a feeling you were going to tell me." At least, he hoped she trusted him that much.

"Maddie and I talked to the doctor today. He wants us to make arrangements to move Mom to a nursing home."

He studied her face. The flicker of joy when she spoke of her brother coming home had vanished.

"Were you surprised by that news?" he asked, carefully neutral until he knew just what she was feeling.

"I guess I shouldn't have been." She turned the tines of her fork on the red-checked tablecloth. "But it feels like giving up. Like admitting that there's no hope."

He touched her fingers lightly with his, and she stopped mutilating the tablecloth.

"If you move her, you can have her closer to you, right? Closer to her family and friends, where people can drop in on her every day?"

"Well, yes, I guess so." She considered that, and the misery seemed to lighten. "If we could have her at a skilled care center somewhere in the county, she would be right in the center of things again."

He nodded, wanting to encourage a cheerful outlook. "I'm no expert, but I'd think the more her surroundings were like home, the better it would be for her."

"But what about the therapy she's been getting at the hospital? I'm not sure what a nursing home provides, but it's probably not on a par with a city hospital."

"It's worth looking into, isn't it? I'd think you could arrange to bring a therapist in to work with her, if necessary, couldn't you?"

She brightened. "That's true. The county health service has therapists on staff."

"There you go." His fingertips brushed hers comfortingly. "You'll see. This will work out all right. Your mother will have a better chance of recovery if she's closer to home."

"You're right." Her smile was brilliant. "Thanks, Landon. You've made me feel better."

The urge to speak, to tell her how much she'd come

to mean to him, was so strong he could barely control it. But he had to control it. Violet was vulnerable now, her life turned upside down by a succession of events that would try anyone. He couldn't put the weight of his emotions on her, as well.

"Any time," he said.

"You know, I'd just been wishing Uncle James were here for me to talk to about it. But you're almost as good as he was in making me feel better."

"Uncle James? I thought you didn't have any relatives."

"James Crawford. He wasn't really our uncle, but we called him that. He owned the ranch when our mother came to Grasslands to work for him."

It looked as if the subject he'd wondered about was coming out into the open without his even asking any questions. "You must have been very close to him."

She nodded, her eyes misty. "He treated us like family. And when he needed help running the ranch, Mom pitched right in. By his last illness, she was pretty much running the ranch. I don't think anyone was surprised when he left the ranch to us. We were the only family he had, even though we weren't blood kin."

Even allowing for Violet's natural bias, the story made sense, and the doubts he'd been harboring about Belle Colby drifted away. Surely nobody could fool the whole community for years, and he hadn't heard anyone say a negative word about Belle since he'd gotten here.

Violet shook her head, seeming to come back from her memories. "Now, about the teen center. You wanted to talk?"

"We're making good progress, but I don't think we can expect to open tomorrow night," he said. "Pastor Jeb suggests having a grand reopening on Saturday evening. If we can put in a full day on Saturday, everything should be ready."

"In other words, you're talking about paying people overtime just to get the work done by Saturday night." She looked troubled, that sense of economy getting the better of her again.

"Look at it this way. If we delay for another week, it gives the kids too much opportunity to fall into other ways of spending their weekends. Right now they're enthusiastic, feeling good about helping get the place back in order. We want to take advantage of that enthusiasm."

Her gaze met his with a softness that nearly made him forget his good resolutions. "All right," she said. "You've given me no arguments left to make. We'll do it your way."

He touched her hand again, ignoring the food in front of him. "You won't be sorry."

The next morning, Violet hurried out toward the corral behind the barn. She wanted to catch Ty before he headed out on his day's rounds. To her surprise, she found Maddie already up and outside, leaning against the board fence that surrounded the corral, watching him. Apparently, Maddie had developed an interest in horses. Or possibly cowboys.

Ty was saddling his favorite horse, and it was impossible to tell from his stoic expression whether he was paying attention to Maddie's banter or not. Maybe it was just as well that she'd come out to interrupt them.

"Enjoying a morning walk?" she asked her twin innocently.

"Something like that," Maddie said, smiling.

"Mornin', Violet." Ty crossed to her, the horse keeping pace with him. "Something you wanted to talk to me about?"

"Good news," she said. "Jack will be home today. And we'll soon be moving my mother to a medical facility closer to home, too."

"That is good news." Ty looked as if a weight had slipped from his shoulders.

"Will you pass that along to all the boys?" she said, her voice casual. "I think they ought to know."

"Yep." His gaze met hers, and she knew he understood her perfectly. "They'll be glad to hear that, for sure." He touched his hat. "See you later, Violet." His gaze slid to Maddie. "Ms. Wallace." He swung into the saddle.

"Maddie," she said.

"Right. Maddie." He shifted his weight slightly. The horse, accustomed to his every move, turned obediently.

Maddie watched him ride away, a bemused expression on her face.

Violet touched her twin's shoulder. "Lupita has breakfast ready."

"Okay." She fell into step with Violet. "Guess I am hungry, at that."

"Going out for an early walk will do that to you," Violet said, amused.

Maddie didn't seem to be paying attention to the teasing. Her forehead wrinkled. "You know, I was thinking maybe I should head back to Fort Worth."

"What?" The comment hit her in the heart. "Why? Maddie, I thought you were happy here."

"I am," Maddie protested. "I'm not talking about going for good. But I left so quickly and there are things I should do. Bills to pay, clothes I should pack…" She shrugged. "Anyway, you'll be busy with Jack coming home, so maybe this is a good time."

Violet caught her arm as they went in the back door, stopping her in the hallway. "You're thinking about leaving because of Jack, aren't you? Because of the way he reacted to seeing you."

"Well, he wasn't exactly thrilled, was he?"

"He was just shocked, that's all," Violet said, struggling to find a middle ground in her loyalty to her siblings.

Maddie wrinkled her nose. "He could have done without having a new sister, believe me."

"I couldn't," Violet said, putting her arm around Maddie's waist. "Now that I know I have a twin, I can't lose you."

Maddie gave her a quick, fierce hug. "Me, too," she said. "Okay. But I will have to go back sometime, you know. There's the little matter of earning a living. I can't just stay here."

"You can stay as long as you want." Jack stepped out from the kitchen with a beaming Lupita right behind him. "It's time I got to know my new little sister, isn't it?"

"Jack." Tears sprang to Violet's eyes, and she threw herself into his arms.

He lifted her off her feet in an enormous bear hug. "Vi, sugar, it's good to see you."

"You, too." She blinked back tears. As he set her on her feet she slugged his shoulder. "That's for staying away so long."

"Yeah. Sorry." His gaze slid away from hers in embarrassment. "That wasn't the most mature thing I ever did, I guess." He turned to Maddie, looking at her a little uncertainly. "Got a hug for your brother, Maddie?"

Maddie smiled, tension easing out of her face. "Sure thing." She held out her arms, and the two of them hugged awkwardly.

That was natural for them to feel ill at ease, wasn't it? It would take time for Maddie and Jack to form a bond. They didn't have what Maddie called the "twin thing" going for them.

It would take time and patience. She just hoped they had enough of each.

Chapter Thirteen

Lupita smiled with joy as she carried more food than they could possibly eat to the table. Obviously, Violet thought, the prodigal son was being welcomed home. Lupita would never admit to playing favorites, but she'd always had an extra-soft spot for Jack.

Maybe that was because Jack and Belle had so often been at loggerheads. Belle had expected a lot of Jack, so frequently reminding him that he was the man of the family.

Perhaps that was why Jack had developed such a need to know who his father was. While Violet had been content with things as they were, Jack had always wanted to know.

Jack had argued with Belle about that very subject the day of her accident. She'd ridden off, furious with him, and he had seen her fall. Small wonder that he'd had such a struggle with the answer to his question falling into Violet's lap.

She and Jack had changed places, it seemed. He didn't want to talk about their parentage, no doubt because he felt so guilty over Belle's accident. And now that she had Maddie in her life, she felt she had to know the rest.

Violet's gaze caught the wise eyes in the portrait of her Uncle James. If he were here, would he know how to deal with this tangled situation?

"Are you really going to eat all that?" Maddie was eyeing Jack's heaped-up plate with amazement.

"You bet," Jack said between forkfuls of burritos filled with Lupita's special scrambled eggs. "I haven't had a decent meal since I left."

An awkward silence fell as all three of them were probably thinking of that night when Maddie had come and Jack had gone. Jack put his fork down and looked at Maddie.

"Listen, Maddie, I'm sorry. I didn't treat you the way I should. When Mom gets better, she'll probably smack me one upside the head for being rude."

"It's okay." Maddie's face relaxed and she grinned at him. "I understand. And if you catch me staring rudely at you, it's just because you're a dead ringer for Grayson."

Violet thought it took an effort, but Jack managed a smile. "So we're as alike as you two are?" He waved his fork between the two of them.

"Identical," Maddie said. "Same brown hair, same eyes." She grinned. "Women are tempted by those golden-brown eyes, you know that?"

Jack shook his head, but Violet laughed.

"He knows," she teased. "He just doesn't want to admit it."

"So when am I going to meet this twin?" Jack wasn't quite convincing in his effort to sound as if he looked forward to that with any enthusiasm.

"I wish I knew. Grayson's a cop. He's doing undercover work right now, and until this case is wrapped up, I can't contact him. He doesn't even know about Mom."

Jack was trying to act as if this were a normal situation, but Violet saw his face tense for a fraction of a second when Maddie referred to Belle that way.

He turned to Violet. "Maybe you'd better tell me more about this business of moving Mom. You sounded pretty upset about it yesterday."

"I was. I guess I still am, but we should have been expecting it. The trauma center is only set up to handle the more immediate care after an accident. I should have realized they'd expect us to move her at some point."

"I don't see why," Jack said. "They're the specialists, aren't they? Isn't that the best place for her to be?"

"That was my reaction, too, at first," she admitted. "But Landon pointed out—"

"Landon? Who's Landon?" Jack was frowning.

How could so much have happened in such a short period of time? It seemed incredible that Jack didn't know Landon.

"Landon is a friend of Maddie's from Fort Worth." She gazed at Maddie, sending her a silent message to keep quiet about whatever she thought of Landon's relationship with Violet. "He's the one who saw me and recognized that we were twins. He's been staying at the hotel for a few days, kind of...helping us out."

"Wait a minute." Jack's frown deepened. "I don't get any of this. What were you doing in Fort Worth to begin with? What kind of a friend is he? A boyfriend?" He looked at Maddie for an answer to that.

"Just a friend," she said easily. "More like a big brother. He's been Grayson's pal since high school."

"I still don't understand why he's hanging around," Jack muttered. "But go on. You were saying something about transferring Mom."

Violet decided to leave Landon's name out of the conversation. His presence was just confusing the issue, and if Jack learned he'd been engaged to Maddie and was now interested in Violet, he'd think...well, she didn't know what he'd think, but it wouldn't be good. And there was certainly no way she could explain her own confused feelings.

Landon was installing a shelf bracket in the games room when he felt someone watching him. He turned and the chair he stood on wobbled.

Violet grabbed it and smiled up at him, making his heart turn over. "Don't you know chairs aren't safe to stand on? You should be using a ladder."

"All the ladders are already in use." He gestured toward the open door to the gym, where Pastor Jeb could be seen putting up new basketball hoops. "Besides, how many times have you stood on a chair to reach something?"

"Too many," she said, making a face at him. "It sounds as if Joe is still working in the restroom."

Actually, prolonged mutters were coming from that direction, where Joe and his helper were setting the new vanity in place.

"I've discovered that it's better to stay away until Joe finishes what he's doing," he said. "Then he wants you to come and admire it."

"Can I admire the shelves in the meantime? They look good. I didn't realize you were working on the project. I mean—" She stopped, maybe thinking that sounded insulting.

He grinned, far from offended. "As opposed to throwing money at the project, you mean? I like to get my hands dirty once in a while."

He tried to lean back to get a view of the shelf and nearly tipped the chair again, so he jumped down. "What do you think? Is it even? We only seem to have one level around here, and someone keeps borrowing it."

Violet stood back, hands on her slim hips, surveying the shelves he'd put up. "Great," she said finally. She swiveled, taking in the whole room—fresh paint on the walls and woodwork, a new Ping-Pong table, the newly painted bookcases. "I can't believe it," she said softly. "I wouldn't have imagined it could look like this after what happened."

"It's amazing what a crew of volunteers can do."

Landon glanced around as well, realizing that he had a more profound sense of satisfaction about this project than about the modern youth center he'd spearheaded in the city. Maybe that was because he'd actually become involved here. He knew the kids who'd enjoy this space. He knew the adults who cared enough to make this happen. And he knew Violet, whose heart was wrapped up in this place.

She looked at him, eyes shining, and in that moment he thought there was nothing he wouldn't do for her.

"I still can't quite believe it. The place looks almost ready to open tonight."

"Not until tomorrow," he said. "Joe promises the restrooms will be ready tomorrow night if he has to work right through supper. And I gather that's a big sacrifice for him." He grinned, trying to defuse the emotion that was building in him. "So tell me, did your brother get home all right?"

She nodded, turning away. "He arrived this morning. Everyone is relieved to have him back. Especially Lupita. I thought she'd never stop cooking. That's her way of expressing love."

But something was wrong—he could hear it in her voice. "What is it?" he asked gently.

She looked at his face, a little surprised, and then she shrugged. "Maybe I was expecting too much from his return. He's really making an effort to get to know Maddie, so that's good. But..." She fell silent.

"But," he prompted.

"I guess I thought he'd be more supportive about moving Mom." She picked up a table-tennis ball and rolled it in her palm. "He doesn't even want to discuss it. He just keeps saying that Maddie and I would know more about that than he would."

He made an effort to suppress his annoyance at a man he hadn't met. "Most men feel helpless when someone they love is sick or hurt." He flashed to a memory of sitting in that hospital corridor for an interminable amount of time, waiting to hear about Jessica. He knew about that helplessness.

"It's not that," Violet said. "Or if it is, that's not the main thing. He was quarreling with Mom right before she had her accident. Demanding to know the truth about our father. That's ironic, isn't it?" Her voice trembled a little. "Anyway, I'm sure he's just feeling so guilty that he hasn't been able to face it."

Landon took her hands in his, wanting to make this better and knowing he couldn't. "I'm sorry," he said. "Give him a little time. He'll come through for you."

She tried to smile. "I hope so. He's a good person, really he is. It's just—" She stopped, as if she couldn't go on.

His fingers moved, caressing her hands. She met his gaze and he saw her eyes darken. Her breath touched him and he leaned closer, ready to feel her lips—

"Hey, Violet, there you are." Sheriff Cole walked into the room, his rolling gait making him look as if he were on the deck of a ship. "Wait until you see what we found."

* * *

Violet turned toward the sheriff, hoping she didn't look as if she'd just been on the verge of being kissed. Or had she? Landon was trying to comfort her—that was in his nature.

She focused on Sheriff Cole. "You found something? Do you know who did it?"

"Knowing's one thing. Proving is another. But we do know something. Come on." He beckoned, and they followed him through the gym and out the door.

Once outside, the sheriff led the way along the building to a narrow passage, about eight feet wide, which ran between this section of the church and the sanctuary.

"There." Sheriff Cole pointed. "Cigarette butts on the ground. Empty beer cans in the basement window well. I'm guessing they gathered in here, drinking and pumpin' themselves up to trash the place."

"You think it was Sam and his buddies, don't you?" She hated to think of the vandals as people she knew. Still, this was Grasslands. Whoever did it, it had to be someone she knew.

"That'd be my guess," the sheriff concurred. "But like I say, proving it is another story."

Landon stirred restlessly. "There would be fingerprints on the cans. DNA, too."

Sheriff Cole stared at him for a moment. "Well, that's true, I reckon. But we don't have the facilities for that sort of thing. We can use the state police lab, but if I told them I wanted to track down three kids for vandalism…well, they'd laugh me out of there in no time flat."

"We don't want to do that anyway," Violet said quickly. "We're trying to show these kids Christian values. We want to give them something to do so they won't turn to beer parties for their entertainment."

"It might be too late for these three," Landon said, looking a little disgruntled. He wanted to fix things, of course. That was what he did.

"It's never too late," she said.

"I don't know." Sheriff Cole shook his head as he stepped back into the sunlight. "Much as I hate to admit it, that kid Sam is a tough one. His dad took off some time ago, and his momma can't seem to keep a rein on that boy."

"Have you asked him about the vandalism?" Landon said.

Violet's thoughts were headed another direction entirely. Could she have handled that situation with Sam any other way? She had to follow the rules, of course. They'd set them up for just such a situation. Still…

"I talked," Sheriff Cole said shortly. "Got nothing but a smart answer for my trouble. Reckon I'll have a word with the other boys' parents, though. Might discourage them from following every dumb idea that Sam Donner has."

Violet nodded, but somehow she doubted that would do much good. The other two boys probably felt like big deals when they followed Sam's lead.

"You know, it might help if we could get someone who's…well, closer to their age, to talk to the kids."

The sheriff patted her shoulder. "You do that, Violet. No harm in getting at the problem from all sides, so to speak. Truth is, though, some kids just have to learn the hard way." Shaking his head, he moved toward his car.

"Pastor Jeb seems to have a good rapport with the kids," Landon pointed out. "Maybe he could talk to them."

"He could," Violet said, wondering how Landon would react to the idea that had popped into her head.

"But I was thinking of someone else. Why don't you talk to them?"

"Me?" Landon stared at her. "I'm no good at things like that. Pastor Jeb's the one you want."

She looked at him steadily. "Pastor Jeb hasn't experienced personal loss that resulted from driving drunk. If you talked to them—"

"No." He took a step back. "I'm sorry, Violet." His voice cracked. "I know you mean well, but I can't do it. Please, forget that idea. Okay?"

There was so much pain in his eyes that she hated herself for having brought it up. "Of course. I'm sorry, Landon."

"It's all right." He forced a smile. "We'd better get back to work."

Chapter Fourteen

Maddie glanced at her watch as they got into the car after their fourth nursing center visit on Saturday afternoon. "I think we'd better call it a day. By the time we get home we'll need to get ready for Teen Scene."

Maddie sounded as down as Violet felt.

"You're right, I guess." She slid into the passenger seat, and Maddie backed out of the lot and headed down the main road.

Violet rubbed her forehead. Good thing Maddie had volunteered to drive on this excursion. As down as she was feeling, she might have run them right off the road.

"Discouraged?" Maddie glanced at her.

"Very. I didn't realize it would be so hard just to find a place that had room for Mom. Let alone one that we like and that has the facilities she needs."

"There are still a few left on our list." Maddie was trying to sound upbeat. "We'll find the right one. I'm sure of it."

"You know, I might have envisioned needing to do this nursing facility search sometime in the very distant future. I sure never thought I'd be doing it at this stage of the game." Violet rubbed her temples again. "And the costs—I had no idea. Of course, Mom didn't think of having insurance that would cover nursing care. She's still a young woman. Why would she?"

"Nobody wants to consider all those somber possibilities," Maddie said. "That's only human nature. But don't worry about the costs. If we find the right place, we'll grab it, regardless of cost. I know Dad will want to help. He'll want her to have the best."

Violet nodded, but in her heart she wondered. They still had no idea what had caused their parents to take such drastic action in splitting them up. Maybe Brian Wallace wouldn't be so eager to rush to his ex-wife's aid.

Had Belle and Brian even been married? They'd been assuming so, based on the original birth certificate for Maddie that Landon's researcher had found. But that was one of the things they still didn't know for sure.

She didn't want to say that to Maddie. One problem was enough at a time. Now they had to find the right place for their mom.

"What about that nursing home next to the clinic in Grasslands? I notice you didn't have it on the list to visit today." Maddie frowned, concentrating on passing a pickup pulling a horse trailer.

"We can stop in there on Monday. It's a nice place—very clean and homelike, and convenient to the clinic right next door. But it's so small. Most of the patients are there because they're elderly and can't take care of themselves anymore, without family that can help. I thought one of the bigger places would be more likely to have the kind of therapy Mom needs."

"Maybe we're not going to find the perfect place." Maddie sighed with resignation. "We'll just have to figure we'll make up for whatever is missing. We can always bring in a therapist to work with her if need be."

"That's what Landon said." Her thoughts shifted to Landon—something they did too frequently these days.

"Speaking of Landon, I gathered you didn't want me to say anything to Jack about your romance." A smile tugged at Maddie's lips.

"It's not a romance," she protested. "Or at least—well, maybe it could be, but everything's so complicated right now. Can you imagine trying to explain to Jack that Landon used to be engaged to you and now he's paying attention to me?" Her head spun at the thought.

Maddie chuckled. "He'd probably head for the horse-whip." She reached across to touch Violet's arm in a comforting gesture. "Sorry. I'm just kidding. Don't listen to me. And don't worry about Jack. Your love life isn't his business, anyway. And Landon can take care of himself."

Those words started a train of thought that Violet didn't welcome. Landon could take care of himself under almost any circumstances, she felt sure of that. He was strong and confident, a man of solid faith and character.

Except in one particular area of his life. His response to her suggestion that he talk to the kids about drunk driving had shown her only too clearly that he hadn't dealt with his sister's death at all.

Or more likely, it was his guilt about her death that he hadn't dealt with.

Landon was a man with an overly developed sense of responsibility. Normally she'd find that admirable. But in this case, she suspected it was crippling him.

Landon made a final check of the restrooms, being sure everything was in order, and walked back through the games room. Funny how this place had become so familiar to him in such a short time. He almost felt as if he belonged here, though the contrast couldn't be greater to the huge church he attended in Fort Worth.

Violet was in the games room, although he couldn't see her face, since she seemed to be looking at something underneath the Ping-Pong table.

"What are you doing?"

She got up quickly, narrowly missing bumping her head. "Landon, I didn't know you were here already. I was just making sure the brackets were secure. In theory there's nothing on this table but the net. But I can't tell you how often I've found kids sitting, leaning, or climbing on it."

"And are they? The brackets, I mean." He moved closer, smiling at her. Her face was flushed from bending under the table, and her hair was escaping from its ponytail. She looked adorable.

"They're fine." She gave the table a little shake. "All is well here, and everywhere else. Maddie's dealing with the kitchen, and aside from the smell of fresh paint, it's ready to go."

"Good." He glanced at his watch and saw that they had a few minutes before the other volunteers started arriving. "How did the nursing home search go today?"

Her expressive face told him, even before she put it in words. "Nothing good enough yet. But we're not giving up. Maddie and I will hit every care facility in the county if we have to. We're going to find it." Those deep brown eyes seemed to darken with worry. "I just wish Jack would get involved. I know he hates to think of Mom sick, but..." She hesitated. "Well, he's my big brother. I know I've always complained because he treated me like a baby, but this is one instance where I'd like to see him taking the lead."

The annoyance Landon had felt over Jack's behavior

bubbled up again. "Big brothers are *supposed* to take the lead." The words came out more harshly than he'd intended. "That's their responsibility."

Violet looked at him, her eyes startled and a little wary at his tone, and he was angry with himself for putting that look on her face.

"Jack's always been good at watching out for me," she said. Naturally she'd defend him. "He just feels so guilty over his quarrel with Mom. He can't help but think that had something to do with her accident."

Landon discovered that he was gritting his teeth to keep from saying what he thought about Jack's actions. Suddenly, he couldn't do it any longer.

"I don't care how you dress it up, Jack's behavior is selfish. He's let you deal with everything while he wallows in his guilt. You shouldn't make excuses for him."

"Wallows?" Violet's voice rose, and the concern in her face turned to anger. "I don't think you have room to criticize Jack for his actions."

"What do you mean? I'm not like Jack." He rejected that idea quickly.

"Aren't you?" Violet planted her hands on her hips. "You've done the very same thing. You've blamed yourself for your sister's death, never giving a thought to all the other people who shared responsibility for what happened. You've let your guilt affect the rest of your life, even planning to settle for a marriage without love, and..."

She stopped abruptly, looking horrified at herself. Probably knowing she'd gone too far.

Landon's heated anger turned cold. He could almost taste the bitterness on his tongue. He'd been fool enough to tell Violet things about himself that he'd never told anyone else, and at the first opportunity, she'd used that knowledge to betray him.

"Landon, I'm sorry. I didn't mean…I shouldn't have…"

Violet was holding out her hand to him, but he turned away. He couldn't stay here any longer.

Heedless of her words, he stalked out.

Violet stood there, gripping the table with both hands. What had she done?

She'd let her shaky emotions get the better of her, said things she shouldn't have, and now Landon was gone.

She took a deep breath, then another, reaching out in silent prayer for strength and clarity. She shouldn't have thrown his own actions back at Landon that way.

But at heart, she knew what she'd said was true. Landon had let his guilt over his sister's death affect every other aspect of his life. Unless he could manage to forgive himself, how could he ever have a deep relationship with anyone?

He couldn't. And after what she'd done, even if he could, it would never be with her.

Now that their relationship was broken beyond repair, she knew just how much she'd grown to love him. She pressed her hand against her heart, trying to deny the pain.

"Violet?" Maddie came in from the kitchen. "What's going on? The volunteers are starting to come in. Where's Landon? I thought he was in here."

Violet blinked rapidly. She wanted to collapse in tears or crawl into a hole and stay there, but she couldn't do either. She had a job to do. No matter how much she hurt, she had to go on.

"We had a quarrel," she said, the words blunt because she had to get them out quickly. "He left."

Maddie reached out to her, obviously wanting to comfort her but probably not knowing how. "What did—" She stopped, cleared her throat, started again. "You don't want to talk about it now. We'll talk later. Listen, if you'd like to go home, we have enough people here to help."

Violet shook her head, knowing she couldn't do that, but loving Maddie for offering. "No, it's all right. I'll be better off here."

"Okay." Maddie's expression was troubled. "But if you change your mind, just let me know."

"I won't." She managed a smile.

Maddie patted her hand. "Everybody quarrels. Don't take it too seriously. Landon will probably be back, ready to make up before you know it."

She nodded, because it was easier to agree than to say what she knew to be the truth. Her relationship with Landon was over before it had a chance to begin. Now she'd have to learn to live without him.

Chapter Fifteen

They'd had more youths than ever at Teen Scene tonight. That surprised Violet. Were they all coming out as a show of support? If so, perhaps the vandals had actually done them more good than harm.

Like Joseph in the Old Testament, telling the brothers who had sold him into slavery in Egypt that though they had meant their action for evil, God had used it for good.

Sometimes it was hard to see God working in a difficult situation…like Belle's injury. So she was glad to be able to rejoice in this one, at least.

A few kids were starting to filter out the door as the clock counted down the time to closing. Headlights from parents' cars passed the windows as rides home appeared to collect the teens.

Violet had managed to keep thoughts of Landon at bay by staying busy, but soon she'd have nothing to do but think and regret.

Violet glanced into the kitchen to see that Maddie and her helper were just about finished clearing up. They'd stopped serving food a half hour before closing, so the kitchen volunteers wouldn't get stuck with cleanup after everyone else had left.

Maddie saw her and waved. Then she came over, scanning Violet's face. "Are you okay?"

"I'm holding up," she said, grateful for the concern. "We had a great turnout tonight."

"Yes. Too bad Landon didn't stick around to see it." Maddie's annoyance with him showed in her voice. "The kids really cleaned us out in the kitchen. Why are they always so hungry?"

"It's the natural state of teenagers," Violet said, trying for a show of cheerfulness she didn't feel. She glanced toward the outside door and frowned. "That's Tracey's father coming in. I wonder why."

She started toward them, seeing Tracey's dad scan the small group of kids who were still playing basketball. Then his look seemed to move on to the knots of chattering girls on the gym balcony. Concern deepened on his face. Obviously, Tracey must not have been ready for pickup at the appropriate time.

She grabbed Maddie's arm. "Look over there—the man in the denim jacket. That's Bob Benton, Tracey's father. Will you tell him I'll go find Tracey and send her out?"

"Sure thing. I'm done here." Maddie waved thanks to her helper and started toward the door.

Violet walked back through the games room, vaguely anxious. It wouldn't be the first time that a parent, tired of waiting, had come in to haul a kid out, but Tracey wasn't careless about things like being where she was supposed to be. If anything, she was overly conscientious, maybe because she was worried about her family. Still, there was a first time for everything, so the saying went.

Violet had been able to find some reassuring information for the girl after she'd confided her worry about being taken back to Mexico by her mother. Still, the attorney she'd talked to had said it wasn't very clear-cut, especially if a parent left the country with a child and then refused to return. At this point, all Violet could do about the situation was pray and try to be available if and when Tracey wanted to talk.

Tracey wasn't in the games room. Reminding the kids who were still playing that it was time to wind things up, Violet crossed into the social room, but it was empty already.

Worry edging along her nerves, Violet looked in the restroom and the adjoining hallway. Empty.

She went back through, automatically checking the other doors, but all seemed as it should be. They had to have more than one exit available, of course, in case of emergency, but the kids knew they were not to go up through the church for any reason, and she hadn't heard the bell that would sound when that door was opened.

She checked the rooms again as she walked back through, her concern growing. By the time she reached Bob Benton, it had reached the level of worry.

Maddie, standing with Tracey's father, turned to her as she approached. "Mr. Benton says Tracey was supposed to meet him at quarter 'til in the parking lot, but she never came."

Violet faced the man, a rough-hewn cowboy type who wore a worried frown at the moment. "Is it possible that Tracey could have misunderstood something about the arrangements, Mr. Benton? Maybe thought she was supposed to ride home with someone else?"

He shook his head. "I always pick her up. Are you telling me she's not here?"

"I've checked all the rooms, but let's not panic. We'll look again, but the first thing to do is see when she checked out." She turned to Harriet, who had been manning the door.

But the older woman was shaking her head already. "I've been over the list a dozen times already, Vi. I've got her checking in at seven-ten, and nothing afterward."

"Maybe you missed her," Bob said.

Harriet might have been offended at the suggestion, but her face softened in sympathy when she looked at him. "I couldn't have, and that's the truth of it," she said. "I haven't left my post for a second in the past hour."

"And I saw her more recently than that," Maddie put in. "She came to the pass-through for a soda, and we chatted a few minutes."

Violet thought about the conversation she'd had with the board in regard to handling just such an emergency. The possibility had seemed so remote then. Now she was glad they'd put policies in place.

"Harriet, call Pastor Jeb. And nobody leaves until you've talked to them in detail about when they last saw Tracey Benton. Those who remember seeing her should wait here in the gym until we have a chance to talk to them. If any parents are upset by that—"

"I'll deal with them." Harriet's expression was grim, and Violet knew no one would get past her.

"Maddie, Bob, we'll start working our way back through the rooms. Check every place, and ask all the kids who are still here if they remember seeing her and who they saw her with. It's always possible she slipped out somehow to go home with a friend." That was the most reassuring thing she could think of to say.

Maddie and Bob Benton nodded, and they split up to work their way from one kid to another in the gym. Leaving the gym to them, Violet went on into the kitchen. Nobody was there, but she checked the pantry just the same. An upset teenage girl might look for a secret spot to cry.

There was nothing in the pantry but brooms and the usual paper supplies. Frustrated, she took another look around and headed back to the games room. She hadn't thought to check the tiny office area, and she should.

Ten minutes later, Violet was no further along than she had been. She went back to rejoin Harriet at the door. As she entered the gym, she saw the other adult volunteers questioning kids. When Violet reached Harriet's table, Pastor Jeb was coming in, with Landon right behind him.

Her heart thudded uncomfortably, but she forced herself to walk toward them. "Pastor Jeb, I'm glad you're here." She nodded toward Landon.

"Maddie called me," Landon said shortly. "She knew I'd want to know. Any news?"

"Nothing. I just don't understand how Tracey could get out of the center without our knowing."

She glimpsed movement from the corner of her eye and realized it was one of the boys Landon had played basketball with. He was looking at Landon, and something in his face told her he wanted to speak to him, but the kid backed away when he saw her watching him.

She nodded toward the boy, her gaze meeting Landon's. "It looks to me as if Tommy Fisher wants to talk to you," she said quietly. "He's bound to be shy about being involved in anything, but if he knows something, he might tell you."

Landon hesitated, as if getting information from a reluctant thirteen-year-old was not something he felt capable of. Then he moved casually toward the boy.

Praying silently, Violet watched them, trying not to let the boy catch her.

Please, Father, if he knows anything that will help us find Tracey, let him open up. Help him to see that her safety is more important than any teenage code of silence.

Landon put his hand on the boy's shoulder, bending over to talk quietly to him. After a moment, the two of them walked toward Violet, Landon's hand still on Tommy's shoulder.

"Tommy says he might be able to help." He patted the boy's shoulder. "You can tell us, whatever it is. You want to help us keep Tracey safe, don't you?"

Tommy nodded, staring down at his frayed sneakers. "I don't want to get nobody in trouble," he mumbled.

Bob Benton seemed to think that was directed at him. "I'm not looking to punish Tracey," he said. "I just want to find her and get her home to her mama."

"Come on, Tommy." Landon urged gently. "You heard. You're not getting her in trouble. You're helping her."

Tommy sniffed, and Violet suddenly realized he was on the verge of tears and didn't want anyone to know. "I heard them talking before Tracey came in." He jerked his head toward the door. "Out in the alley."

"Heard who?" Landon urged. "Who was Tracey with?"

Tommy sniffed again. "Sam. Sam Donner."

Violet heard the sudden intake of Landon's breath and saw him stiffen. He was undoubtedly thinking what she was. What if Sam had been drinking?

"What were they going to do?" she asked. "How did Tracey get out of the building?"

A tear slid down one cheek, out of Tommy's control. "I heard him tell her to go out that back door that goes into the church. He done somethin' to the bell so it wouldn't ring. Said it'd be a good joke. He'd be waiting in his car, and they'd go for a ride."

"Had he been drinking?" Landon's voice was incredibly harsh, and Tommy recoiled.

"It's okay, Tommy," she said quickly. "You can tell us."

"I dunno. Maybe." He shrugged, studying his sneakers again.

"Do you have any idea where they were going on this ride?" Her thoughts ran rapidly over the places where teens were known to congregate.

"That's all I know, honest, Ms. Vi. Can I go? My mom's gonna skin me if I'm not home on time."

"That's okay, Tommy. You can go home now." She touched his shoulder lightly, wanting to ruffle his hair but knowing he'd think himself too old for that gesture. "You were a big help. If your mom gives you grief about being late, I'll tell her what happened, okay?"

Tommy nodded and then bolted away from them. But he stopped at the door. "I hope Tracey's okay," he said, and darted out into the dark.

"We'll have to start looking for them," Pastor Jeb said. "If that boy's been drinking, Tracey shouldn't be in a car with him."

"If I catch up with him, he's not gonna be going with any girls in cars for a while." Bob Benton's big hands curled into fists.

"We need to get moving," Landon said abruptly. "Go in pairs, so one person can drive while the other one looks for any sign of them."

Pastor Jeb nodded. "Right. Harriet, you'd best call Sheriff Cole and get his people out. You can send the rest of these kids home. Now pair up, everyone."

"Violet, can you come with me?" Landon's voice was

as impersonal as if she were a stranger. "I don't know the area, and you do."

A thousand reasons why that wasn't a good idea crowded Violet's mind, but Tracey's safety was more important than her feelings. She nodded and followed him out to his car.

By the time they were pulling out of the lot, other duos had started getting into cars. She glimpsed Harriet at the gym door, talking to a group of concerned parents. If she knew her town, there would soon be a number of people out looking.

Tracey would undoubtedly find it embarrassing that half the town knew what she'd done, but that was part of living in a place like this—you didn't get any anonymity. But you did get a lot of people who cared what happened to you.

"Which way?" Landon said, his voice clipped.

"Turn right, then right again. We'll head out to Blue Lake. That's a popular place for kids to go and park."

He followed her directions without comment, but by the time he was on the road out of town, he couldn't seem to keep quiet any longer. "What would possess her to go off with a boy like Sam? You'd think she could see him for what he is."

At least he was accepting the fact that Tracey bore some responsibility for her actions, which was more than he'd done in regard to his sister. Did he realize the dichotomy in his attitude?

"Tracey's been vulnerable lately. She probably liked the attention from an older boy. Girls do stupid things sometimes, even though they know it's wrong."

"Vulnerable how?"

"Tracey hasn't told me the whole story, but I do know

her parents have been fighting. She asked me if she'd have to go back to Mexico if her mother wanted to go."

Landon shot a look at her. "You didn't tell me that."

"There wasn't anything you could do, and she only told me on my promise to keep quiet. Which I'm breaking." She shook her head. "But this situation is too serious for keeping secrets now."

Landon nodded, his profile stern in the dim light. "How much farther is it?"

"There's a turnoff to the right about a mile down the road. It's just a lane, so you'd better slow down."

Landon's hands were tight on the wheel, but he slowed down as she'd said. Soon she spotted the end of a fence that marked the lane.

"There—right where that white post is." She gripped the door handle as he turned down the narrow, rutted lane. "If they are there, what are we going to do? We can't force Tracey to go with us."

"She'll come." Landon's tone was faintly threatening.

They bounced in a rut, Violet's head nearly hitting the roof of the car. Just as she thought her bones were going to shake apart, they emerged onto the roughly cleared space that overlooked the small, man-made lake.

As she might have imagined, there were three vehicles parked there, spaced apart. She eyed them quickly. "I don't think they're here. Sam drives a beat-up, old black pickup."

"He could have borrowed a car." Landon slid out, taking a flashlight. "Are you coming?"

Obviously she was. They approached the first car, Violet feeling a bit of trepidation.

At least the kids in the car didn't react violently when Landon tapped on the window with his flashlight. The driver rolled the window down.

"We're not—" he began, and then stopped. "What's going on, man? You're not the cops."

"I'm looking for Sam Donner. Have you seen him?"

The boy's gaze slid away from Landon's. "Can't say as I have."

Violet stepped forward into the light. "Jesse Halstrom. I'm surprised to see you here." She waited a second, letting him register the fact that not only did she know him, she had been his Sunday School teacher last year. "What were you saying about Sam Donner?"

Jesse cleared his throat. "Hey, Ms. Vi. I…I was just going to say that I spotted that rattletrap he calls a truck headed down Goose Hollow Road maybe an hour or so ago. Going way too fast."

Landon headed for his car. "Come on."

"Thank you, Jesse." Violet hurried after him.

Landon took the road Violet indicated, trying not to let his anxiety affect the pressure of his foot on the gas pedal. They wouldn't do anyone any good if they had an accident.

Violet was on her cell phone talking to the reverend, who was coordinating the search. "All right. Thanks, Pastor Jeb. We'll be in touch." She cut the connection.

"Any news from the search party?"

"Nothing yet. So far we seem to be the only ones with a lead."

He nodded. "How far ahead is this road?"

"About another mile."

Something about Violet's voice made him glance at her. "Aren't you sure?"

"I'm sure about where the road is," she said. "I'm just wondering if we're scaring ourselves unnecessarily. After all, we don't have any proof that Sam's been drinking."

"Are you willing to take that chance?" he demanded.

"No, of course not. I guess I'm just trying to find some hope to cling to. Even if Sam was drinking, that doesn't mean he'll have an accident."

So she knew that was his fear. He gritted his teeth, never wanting to live through that particular pain again. Tracey wasn't his sister, but he'd still feel he'd failed her if the worst happened.

"You couldn't have known this was going to happen," Violet said, as if she knew what he was thinking. "You don't know these kids anywhere near as well as I do, and I had no idea Tracey was interested in Sam Donner."

He glanced at her, hearing the guilt in her voice. "You couldn't have known, either, Violet. Don't beat yourself up over it." The anger he'd felt toward her earlier was subsiding, drowned in the more immediate emergency.

"There's the turn," she said, leaning forward and pointing.

He swung into the road. It pitched sharply downward, the trees thick on either side. It was like falling into a well. He couldn't see anything except the short stretch of road within range of his headlight beams.

"This is a terrible road." Violet stated the obvious. "Better slow down—" Her voice choked on the word.

And then he saw what she had, and his own throat seemed to close. A vehicle, off the road, half in a gully, hood against a tree, its headlamps slanting upward to stab the sky.

Chapter Sixteen

Landon was out of the car almost before he'd brought it to a stop, leaving the door swinging. Violet grabbed her cell phone, calling 911 as she ran toward the pickup. She rattled off the directions, reaching Landon's side with the dispatcher's assurances ringing in her ears.

"They're on their way," she said. "Tracey?"

"I can't see her." Landon handed her the flashlight and yanked at the door. It stuck, and he braced his foot against the frame and pulled. The door shrieked and opened.

Heart pounding, wordless prayers forming, Violet aimed the flashlight beam into the truck.

Sam Donner blinked against the light, blood trickling from a gash on his head. He groaned. "Wha…wh…"

Violet could smell the beer from outside the pickup. She flashed the light over the rest of the interior. Tracey wasn't there.

"If she was thrown out—" Landon muttered, fear in his voice. He grasped Sam's shoulder. "Where's Tracey? Answer me. What happened to Tracey?"

Violet caught his hand, his pain pummeling her as

well. Landon was reliving his sister's death—how could he help it in circumstances like this?

"Don't, Landon." She pulled his hand away. "We don't know how badly he's injured. Let me."

For a moment she thought Landon wasn't even hearing her. Then he stepped back and she edged past him.

She touched Sam's cheek, fearful of a head injury. He wasn't in immediate danger of being hurt worse, so they probably shouldn't try to move him.

"Sam," she said urgently. "Sam…listen to me. Where's Tracey?"

"T-Tracey?" he muttered.

"Tracey Benton. You left the church with her. Where is she? Was she in the truck with you?"

He didn't answer. This was useless—they should start searching. Where would Tracey be if she'd been thrown out?

"Where is she?" Landon demanded. He sounded as if he had control of himself again.

Sam seemed to rouse. "Tracey." He frowned, his head moving side to side. "Said I was drunk. I'm not. Let her out."

A wave of relief swept through Violet. "Where, Sam?" She patted his cheek. "You're hurt, but the ambulance is on its way. Now tell us where Tracey got out so we can find her." She could already hear the siren, coming ever closer.

Sam's eyes closed. If he didn't answer they'd be left searching the county for Tracey, not knowing…

"Jenkins' Mill," he muttered. "She got out."

"Where's Jenkins' Mill?" Landon growled. "She's out there by herself. Anything could happen."

Violet wanted to protest that this was Grasslands, not the city, but bad things could happen anywhere. She stepped back as the sheriff's car, siren wailing, pulled up, closely followed by the EMTs.

"The mill is on the edge of town. We'll find her."

A few minutes later they were back in Landon's car headed for town, leaving Sam in the capable hands of the EMTs.

"At least this might force Sam to get the help he needs," she said.

Landon's hands tightened on the wheel, and she knew he was seeing the boy who'd been responsible for his sister's death instead of Sam. Fresh pain pierced her heart. What could she say to him?

"Let's hope so," he said finally. "We're almost at the edge of town. Keep looking along the road."

Landon slowed the car, and she focused on the area ahead of them, watching for any sign of movement. No one seemed to be out in this area at night—it was mostly businesses, closed at this hour.

They were nearing the church when she grabbed Landon's arm. "Look, there. In the doorway of the flower shop."

Landon braked, stopping at the curb. Tracey huddled forlornly against the flower shop door, arms wrapped around herself.

Thank You, Lord. Violet slid out and approached Tracey, struggling to get her voice under control before she spoke.

"Hey, Tracey." She put her arm around the girl. "It's all right. We're so glad to find you."

Landon approached cautiously. "Are you okay, Tracey?"

Tracey nodded, wiping tears away with her palms. "I...I'm sorry. I didn't know what to do."

Violet hugged her. "It sounds to me as if you did just

right. You realized Sam had been drinking and you made him let you out."

"I'm so ashamed." A fresh bout of tears flowed. "I sneaked out of Teen Scene and now you'll never let me back in again. It was too far to walk home, and I couldn't find any place open to call. I was afraid to go to a house where I didn't know the people…and I didn't know what to do!"

The litany ended on a wail, and Tracey buried her face in Violet's shoulder and sobbed.

Violet couldn't help but smile at Landon even as she tried to comfort the girl. The recital was such a mixture of woes that she didn't know where to begin dealing with it.

Landon's face was unreadable in the dim light. He pulled out his cell phone.

"Listen, Tracey." She held the teen by both shoulders. "You made a mistake, okay? And you're sorry. You handled it well, once you knew you were in too deep. That's the important thing. Now Mr. Derringer is going to let the people who are searching know you're okay, and then we're going to take you home."

Tracey's lips trembled. "Daddy will yell, and Mama will cry, and—"

"I promise, if they do, it's only because they were scared to death something bad happened to you." She kept her tone firm and practical, sensing that was the best way to deal with Tracey's overflowing emotions. "Come on now." She piloted the girl to the car.

Landon slid behind the wheel. "The sheriff is calling off the search party, and Tracey's father will meet us at their house."

"What about Sam?" she asked.

Tracey leaned forward in the backseat, distracted from her own misery. "Did something happen to Sam?"

"He wrecked his truck," Landon said. "The EMTs took him to the hospital, but they don't think it's anything serious."

"I told him he shouldn't be driving. Maybe, if I hadn't got out, he wouldn't have crashed."

"Don't think that way." Landon spoke sharply, probably out of his own memories. "You did the right thing. If you hadn't gotten out of that pickup, you'd be the one on the way to the hospital. Or maybe the morgue."

"Landon..." Violet intervened.

"It's true, and Tracey needs to understand that." He was uncompromising. "Listen to me, Tracey, because I know what I'm talking about. My sister Jessie was just about your age when she got into a car with a boy who was drunk. But she didn't have your common sense. She didn't get out, and she died because of that. So don't ever think it would have made a difference if you'd stayed."

He'd actually spoken of his sister. Violet's emotions tumbled and she fought to stay in control.

"I...I'm sorry." Tracey's voice was very small. "About your sister."

Landon nodded, and they rode the rest of the way to the mobile home park where Tracey lived in silence, except for the necessary directions.

Violet studied Landon's face as they went up the walk with Tracey, but he had his stoic mask on, not giving anything away. This night had put his deepest grief through the wringer, and she wasn't sure how he was going to react to that. He must be tempted just to get into his car and hightail it back to Fort Worth, in order to forget she and this place ever existed.

* * *

Landon declined the second cup of coffee that Maria Benton tried to force on him. He was never going to sleep tonight as it was. He'd have headed out once they'd delivered Tracey to her parents, but Violet clearly had something on her mind.

Now Violet sat on the threadbare couch, reaching out to pat Tracey's hand where she sat with her mother's arm around her. "I'm sure you'd like for us to get out of here," she said. "But I think there's something we should bring out into the open before anything else happens."

Tracey's parents exchanged glances. "I don't understand," Maria said. "Tracey was very foolish, but she's okay now."

Violet leaned toward the girl, her gaze on Tracey's face. "You need to talk to your parents, Tracey. Tell them what you've been worried about."

"Tracey?" Bob Benton touched his daughter's cheek lightly. "Honey, what's wrong? What's Ms. Vi talking about?"

Tracey shook her head, lips pressed together. Then the tears started to flow again.

"I heard you arguing." Tracey looked at her mother. "I heard you saying about going back to Mexico. I don't want to. I don't want to leave Daddy and my friends… and my school."

Landon could see by the parents' expressions that they had no idea Tracey had overheard them.

Bob Benton sat down on the coffee table in front of his daughter, taking her hands in his. "Tracey, honey, you've got it all wrong. We weren't talking about splitting up." He looked at his wife. "You have to tell her the truth."

Maria's dark eyes, so like Tracey's, were brimming with tears, but she nodded. "I love you and your daddy," she said softly. "I love our lives here. But a piece of my heart is still in Mexico." She stroked her daughter's hair. "You see, I have another daughter. Your half sister. She is almost eighteen now, and I haven't seen her in so long. It tears my heart to bits to think of her never knowing you."

Tracey's eyes were round. "But…you never told me."

Maria wiped her eyes. "I was afraid if you knew I had left her behind with her grandparents that you would be afraid I could do that to you. I thought I was doing what was best."

Secrets. Landon glanced at Violet. Secrets had torn her family apart, and only the good Lord knew if that could ever be made right.

"I have a sister." Tracey seemed to be trying the words on for size. "What's her name? What does she look like? Why can't she come here and be with us?"

"Miranda," her mother answered. "Her name is Miranda. She lives with my parents, and they are Mama and Papa to her. She would like to come here, maybe go to school, but the immigration…" She stopped. "It's so hard, and it takes money."

Pain tightened Bob's face. "I'd do it if I could, honey. You know that. But we're barely getting by as it is."

Landon's hands tightened on his knees. He had been so blessed financially that it seemed unfair when others had so little. But he could at least help with part of the Benton family's problem.

"The foundation I work with has a good immigration lawyer," he said. "He deals with things like this all the time. Will you let me contact him for you?"

"We don't take charity—" Bob began.

"Not charity," he said hastily. He'd seen that kind of pride before, and he admired it. "But the attorney will do the work up front, and you can pay him back over time. It would be like a school loan for Miranda. Most kids get those now."

The stubborn pride melted from Bob's face as he looked at his wife. "We…we'd be awful grateful."

"No need," Landon said, rising. "I'll be headed back to Fort Worth tomorrow, and the lawyer's office will be in touch for the information they need sometime next week. Okay?"

Bob nodded. Tracey and her mother were both crying again. Landon looked at Violet and nodded toward the door. There was nothing more they could do here, but with any luck, Tracey and her family were going to be all right.

He wasn't so sure about himself. His emotions had been turned inside out by everything that had happened. He needed time to sort everything out, time to be sure that what he was feeling for Violet was real.

He thought about what Violet had said to him…the truth that had come out when she was angry. Maybe, real or not, it was too late.

Sunday morning. Landon had heard the church bells ringing from his hotel room. He should have gone to church. Or he should be on the road back to Fort Worth.

He didn't want to do either of those things. He wanted to see Violet, to tell her what he felt. The trouble was that after a mostly sleepless night, he didn't seem to be any closer to an answer now than he had been before.

Finished dressing, he picked up his suitcase and walked down the stairs. Maybe going back to Fort Worth was the best solution. Once he was busy with his normal routine, maybe his feelings for Violet would take their proper proportion.

He'd reached the car and was putting his case in the

back when he realized people were coming out of the church down the street. Violet's church. If she saw him...

But it wasn't Violet who was walking quickly toward him. It was Maddie.

She reached him, slightly out of breath, and let her gaze shift from him to the suitcase and back again. "Going somewhere, Landon?"

He definitely didn't want to talk to Maddie about his feelings for Violet. "I have work waiting for me back at the office. And now that your brother is here, you don't need me."

Maddie raised her eyebrows. "If I didn't see it with my own eyes, I wouldn't believe it. Landon Derringer, running away."

"I'm not running away." He tried to grab hold of his temper before it cut loose. "I just think it's for the best if I leave. Besides, you're the one who keeps telling me to butt out of your business. I should think you'd be glad to see the back of me."

"Maybe, maybe not." She tilted her head to the side, looking at him as if she hadn't seen him before. "What's more important to me right now is how Violet feels. Have you even said goodbye to her?"

He turned away, slamming the trunk lid. "I'll be in touch. I just think—"

"You just think you might actually have to risk showing your feelings if you hang around here any longer," Maddie snapped. "Well, go ahead, if that's the most important thing to you. But you'd better think about what you'll be losing if you drive away now. It might be more than you're willing to risk."

He opened his mouth to respond, but it was too late. Maddie was striding off down the street, anger showing in every click of her heels.

Landon got into the car, venting a little temper of his own by slamming the door. Maddie might think she had the right to meddle, but she didn't. This was between him and Violet, and he wasn't going to jump into anything until he was sure he was right.

That temper lasted him about ten miles down the road toward Fort Worth. Then he slowed. And stopped, hands grasping the wheel. He stared out at the rolling grasslands on either side of the road, but all he could see was Violet's face, all he could hear was her voice.

Running away, Maddie had said. He was running away rather than facing the risk of showing his feelings. Was that really the way he wanted to live his life?

Little Maddie had done some growing up since she'd met her twin. She was no longer the kid who'd cried over her lost job and said yes to marriage because she didn't know what else to do with her life.

And maybe, just maybe, she knew what she was talking about. He pressed on the gas, turning the car in the middle of the empty road, and headed back toward the Colby Ranch.

Chapter Seventeen

Violet heard a car coming down the lane. Lupita would have Sunday dinner on the table in a few minutes. Who would be coming to call now?

She leaned toward the window to look out, and her heart nearly stopped. It was Landon.

Maddie glanced over her shoulder, and then gave her a smile that looked rather like the expression of a satisfied cat. "He's here to see you, not me. Better go out and meet him. I'll make sure no one bothers you."

She sent an accusing glance at her sister. "What did you do?"

"Nothing." Maddie sounded way too innocent. "Go on, now." Maddie gave her a push toward the door.

By the time Violet reached the porch, Landon was getting out of his car. He stood for a moment, looking at her with an expression she couldn't interpret. Then he came quickly to her.

"Is there someplace we can talk? Alone?"

If he'd come to tell her he was going to Fort Worth and not coming back, she'd better hear it with no one else around. "Let's walk over toward the pecan groves. It'll be cooler under the trees."

She led the way, and Landon walked beside her, not speaking. The longer the silence stretched, the more difficult it would be to speak at all.

And how could she say anything, even if she could find the words? Last night Landon had basically walked out of her life. Did she dare to believe that anything had changed?

They reached the shadow of the trees, and Landon turned to face her.

She took a breath. "Landon, I'm sorry. What I said about your grief—it was inexcusable. I shouldn't—"

He put his finger on her lips, silencing her. He was very close in the dimness under the trees.

"Don't, Violet. Don't be sorry, because everything you said was true."

"I was still unkind to say it. I had no right to strike back at you that way."

"You had to." His hand moved, the back of his fingers gentle against her cheek. "I wasn't seeing it for myself, was I? I've spent all these years rejecting God's forgiveness, trying to make up for losing Jessie by sponsoring charities, but never letting my heart be touched." He shook his head. "Until I came here, and started to see what helping people really meant. Not just throwing money at a problem, but putting your heart on the line."

She couldn't let him denigrate the good he'd done. "You've helped so many people, Landon. No matter what your motives were, you helped them. That's important."

He was shaking his head again, but this time she thought it was in wonderment at himself.

"Ever since I met you in that coffee shop, you've been turning my perceptions upside down. You've been hammering my locked heart open. And yesterday—" He stopped, and a shudder went through him.

She spoke quickly, not wanting him to relive it. "It was a close call, but Tracey is fine. Maybe this will even be the wake up Sam needed. And with your help, the Benton family will be all right. That's a pretty good payoff for all the worry we went through." She tried to smile, hoping to relieve the pain she feared still lurked inside him.

"Tracey took care of herself. She did the right thing. If Jessie had done that, she'd be alive today."

"You can't change the past," she said, her voice gentle. He was referring to his sister by her nickname now, she noticed, as if he could open up his memories to the child she'd been long ago.

"You're right." He touched her face again, and his fingers were warm on her cheek. "Neither of us can do that, any more than the Bentons can. All we can do is forgive and move on."

She put her hand over his, pressing his palm against her skin. "If you can do that now, then everything has been worth it. Even if…"

"Even if what?" Landon leaned closer.

"You…you said you were going back to Fort Worth." She didn't want the pain to show in her voice, but it did.

"Not for good," he said quickly. "Not unless you want me to stay away."

Her heart seemed to have gotten stuck on the fact that he was coming back, and it was singing so loudly in her ears that she could barely think. "I…I don't."

"I thought I needed time," he said. He took both her hands, holding them between his as solemnly as if they were making a vow. "But your sister told me I was running away because I was afraid to risk showing my feelings. Maybe she was right. Maybe that was why I was so eager to keep everyone at arm's length, why I was even ready to settle for a marriage without love."

He was quoting her words back to her. "I'm sorry. I shouldn't have said that. I didn't mean to hurt you."

Landon dropped a kiss on her fingertips. "It was worth any hurt it caused me, because it made me look at myself. You and Maddie between you made me see what I was doing. I'm ready to take the risk now. I know it hasn't been very long, but when it's right, you know it. I love you, Violet, more than I can say."

Her heart seemed to be beating somewhere up in her throat, and she could swear she heard songbirds singing in the trees. But maybe that was just the sheer joy that was rushing through her. She looked into his face, seeing the love that shone in the depths of his eyes, and she knew it was for real.

"I love you, Landon." She would say more, but his lips closed on hers. Tenderness flowed through her, seeming to touch every cell of her body. His arm went around her, holding her close. She had never felt so cherished, so loved.

Finally, Landon drew back, still holding her in his arms. His face was so open and relaxed that her breath caught. This was how he looked with all the barriers down.

"I hate to say it, but I do have to go back to Fort Worth for a day or two. I have to deal with some business and get the immigration attorney started on the Benton situation," Landon went on, not waiting for a comment. "And there's something I have to show you."

"Show me?" She looked up at his face, puzzled.

"Something that comes with a confession. You know that photo of your family that I had enhanced for you?"

She nodded, bemused at the change of subject.

"Guess I was being a little overprotective," he said. "Annoyingly so, I think you could say."

"What did you do?" It surely couldn't be anything that bad.

"The enhanced photo brought up an address on the mailbox. An address in Fort Worth. I was afraid you and Maddie would rush off half-cocked and get yourselves hurt, so—"

"So you deleted it on our copies." She glared at him, but he looked so contrite that her heart wasn't in it. "Interfering. Bossy. Annoying," she said.

"Guilty on all counts. Forgive me?" He leaned closer, so near that his warm breath touched her cheek.

"As long as you promise not to hide anything else from me for my own good," she said firmly.

"I promise." His lips brushed hers. "As long as you promise to include me in any plans you make for the future."

That was an easy promise to make, Violet knew as his lips found hers again. She wrapped her arms around him, holding him close. Their lives had taken some odd twists and turns, and all of those hadn't been unraveled yet. But God had brought them through to the place they really belonged—with each other.

Epilogue

"Let me see it again." Maddie grabbed Violet's hand to admire the ring Landon had given her. "That Landon doesn't waste any time, does he?"

"That's what Jack keeps saying." Violet pulled riding gloves on, hiding the ring for the moment. "'You've only known him a month. Why do you want to get engaged?' But when you know it's real, you know."

"I guess so." Maddie sighed. "It makes me think I'm missing something. Something I never felt with Landon."

Violet smiled at her twin. "It will happen for you. I know it. Now, if we're going to go for a ride this morning, we'd best get moving."

Maddie nodded. "I think we have a few too many things on our to-do lists. Decide on the right nursing facility, follow up that clue to the house in Fort Worth, to say nothing of renovating the guesthouse so that it's suitable for a newly married couple..."

Violet nodded, glancing toward the guest cottage. According to Landon's plans, it would soon be doubled in size. Her heart seemed to swell at the thought of living there with him.

"I'm just so relieved that Landon doesn't want me to

ove to Fort Worth. Given Mom's situation, I wouldn't want to be that far away, and there's the produce business to run, as well."

"Landon has telecommuting down to a fine art, as far as I can tell," Maddie said. "Even if he has to go into the city every week or so, at least this way you don't have to give up your work. Speaking of which, it's about time I started looking for my next job, whatever it's going to be."

"I wish you didn't have to leave here to find it." They had gotten so close in the last month. Violet hated to think of being without her.

But Maddie didn't seem to be listening. She was looking toward one of the small barns, her hand shielding her eyes from the sun. "Who is that with Ty Garland?"

Violet followed the direction of her gaze. Ty was there, all right, standing by one of the pens that contained a sow and her babies. But there was a child with him.

"I guess we'd better find out." She headed for Ty with Maddie right beside her.

Ty looked up at their approach. "Violet. Maddie." He nodded, his normally stoic face very tense.

"Morning, Ty. Who's this?" Violet watched the little girl, who looked about eight or so, approach the pen and then turn away, wrinkling her nose.

"Sorry I didn't have a chance to talk to you about her, Violet. That's Darcy. My little girl."

Violet hoped her face didn't show how shocked she was. She'd known that Ty had been married—a marriage that ended when his wife left him. She'd never heard anything about a child.

"She's adorable," Maddie gushed. Not knowing what a surprise this was, Maddie could sound perfectly normal in her response. "With that brown hair and brown eyes, she looks just like you, Ty."

Ty nodded. "Guess she does, at that." He sounded faintly surprised, as if that hadn't occurred to him.

The little girl—Darcy—had wandered along the fence, tapping it with a stick as children always seemed to do. Ty looked as if to be sure she was out of earshot, and then he turned back to them.

"Thing is, I never even knew I had a kid. My ex-wife made sure of that." Bitterness threaded his voice. "Now she's gone and I'm left with a kid I don't know who's never been out of a city in her life. What am I going to do with her?"

Violet's heart was touched by his turmoil, and she could see that Maddie felt the same. "You're her father. She'll feel a connection with you. That's what's important now. We'll all help her feel at home here. And once school starts, she'll have friends and new activities."

"I s'pose. Kids have gone through worse and come out okay, I guess," he conceded. "But I can't work and watch her at the same time until school starts. And where am I going to find a good sitter who can take care of her on such short notice?"

The idea popped into her head with such ease it was as if it was meant. "What about Maddie?" she proposed. "She's here, and she was just saying that she wanted a job."

Maddie's eyebrows lifted. "That wasn't exactly the kind of job I had in mind." But she was smiling at the little girl.

"You're great with kids," Violet reminded her. "I've watched you with them at Teen Scene. It's the perfect answer. You'd be helping Ty, and it means you'd stay here for a while longer, at least. I'm not ready to lose my twin yet."

Maddie's smile turned to a mischievous grin. "I'm in. But it's possible Ty doesn't want me."

They both looked at Ty. He seemed torn between emotions, doubt about Maddie battling relief at the simple answer to his problem. "I guess we could give it a test run. Maybe until school starts, anyway."

"It's a deal," Maddie said promptly.

Violet could breathe again. She wasn't going to lose her twin. With Maddie here, together they could work on the fragile bond that was beginning to weave their family back together at last.

* * * * *

Look for Maddie's story,
MIRROR IMAGE BRIDE
by Barbara McMahon, coming soon.

Dear Reader,

Thank you for picking up this first installment of the brand-new Texas Twins series. All the authors hope you enjoy our stories as much as we've enjoyed working together to write this series for you.

I was especially pleased to be writing a book about twin sisters who discover each other. I was the youngest by a number of years in my family, and when I was young I always imagined what it would be likc to have a sister who was exactly my age.

I hope you'll let me know how you felt about this story. I'd love to send you a signed bookmark or my brochure of Pennsylvania Dutch recipes. You can write to me at Love Inspired Books, 233 Broadway, Suite 1001, New York, NY 10279, email me at marta@martaperry.com, or visit me on the web at www.martaperry.com.

Blessings,

Marta Perry

Questions for Discussion

1. Can you understand the conflict Violet faced when she discovered that she had a secret twin? Have you ever found that something joyful can also have a sorrowful side, as Violet did when she struggled to understand her parents' decision?

2. Landon is a man guided by his sense of responsibility, but that admirable quality led him into a mistake when he proposed to Maddie. Can you think of other examples of times when a good quality might lead someone into a mistake?

3. Violet finds that building a relationship with her newfound sister can have both problems and strengths. Have you found that dealing with troubles can sometimes bring a family closer together? Why or why not?

4. Violet's growing dedication to her sister gives her the courage to bring their situation out in the open, despite the gossip it might involve. Have you ever experienced the effects of gossip? If so, explain.

5. Landon helps other teenagers through his foundation in his sister's memory, but he hasn't dealt with his grief and guilt. What experiences have you had of God's help in time of grief? Is there anything that you tend to hold back from God?

6. The scripture verse for this story is a familiar one, but it packs some powerful meaning in a few

words and it emphasizes God's incredible power and care for us. What meaning does this verse have for you?

7. Violet's sister finds a community and acceptance at the Colby Ranch, even though it's very different from her life in Fort Worth. Have you had the experience of feeling like a fish out of water in a new place? Who made you feel welcome?

8. Both Violet and Landon are challenged to be honest about their problems. Do you think we turn to God more readily when times are difficult? Why or why not?

9. Violet finds comfort and strength in worshipping together with her church. Do you find that in your church? Or do you find it elsewhere?

10. How does Landon respond when he's pushed into dealing personally with the teenagers? Can you understand his hesitation and doubt?

11. Has God ever called you to serve Him in a way that wasn't comfortable for you? How did you cope with that?

12. When you have an opportunity to welcome someone new to your church or community, how do you do that?

13. Which character in the story did you feel was living the most Christlike life? Why?

14. Is it most difficult to be honest with yourself about your fears and shortcomings, or to be honest with someone else? Why?

15. Does the story give you the sense that the twins will overcome the loss of their childhood together? How do you think it will affect their lives?

COMING NEXT MONTH from Love Inspired®

AVAILABLE JULY 31, 2012

A HOME FOR HANNAH

Brides of Amish Country

Patricia Davids

When former Amishwoman Miriam Kauffman finds a baby on her doorstep, she's forced to work with Sheriff Nick Bradley...which means facing their past.

MIRROR IMAGE BRIDE

Texas Twins

Barbara McMahon

Thrown off-kilter by the discovery of family members they never knew, Maddie Wallace and Ty Garland form a connection as she nannies for his daughter.

HER HOMECOMING COWBOY

Mule Hollow Homecoming

Debra Clopton

After her sister dies, Annie Ridgeway must find her nephew's father and introduce him to his son—but is bull rider Colt Holden cut out to be a daddy?

THE RANCHER'S SECRET WIFE

Cooper Creek

Brenda Minton

Before leaving for the amy, Reese Cooper married pregnant dancer Cheyenne Jones to secure her future—when she returns to his life, can Reese provide lasting security for her?

THE BACHELOR BOSS

Judy Baer

Caring for Tyler Matthews' sick grandmother is the job Hannah St. James signed up for, but soon she finds herself caring for the overworked businessman, too!

LAKESIDE FAMILY

Lisa Jordan

Single mother Josie Peretti will do anything to save her sick daughter's life—even if it means contacting high-school sweetheart Nick Brennan, who broke her heart.